Faunication: Kali's Story
by Yamila Abraham

Dear Friends, please don't share this ebook online! Piracy has devastated my ability to make a living in the past. I beg you to please not post this or any of my works online. Thanks so much to everyone who has supported me with a legal purchase!

1 Cousin

Since I'm writing this book for humans, I won't say how old I was when I had sex with my cousin. What fauns consider play was usually pantomiming lovemaking, even when we're barely beyond middle school.

My cousin George was the same age as I, and we'd both inherited the attractive traits of our lineage. He had white ringlets of hair, vivid blue eyes, and lips so red you'd think he'd colored them with berry juice.

I was said to be as handsome as he, but I wasn't sure. Older relatives doted on me, claiming I would one day grow up to be a gorgeous faun lord, but that's what aunts and uncles did. I didn't trust their opinions.

Still, I was suitable enough for George, and, neither of us having any siblings, we adopted each other. We played the way human children often do in the early grades of school. After that we both suffered confusing lust and had only each other to experiment with. It's not as though we were in love, because we were too young to understand such things, but puberty brought upon the burgeoning desires common to all fauns.

Our game was to pretend to be married, and we'd rub against each other on the soft grass behind our grandfather's barn. Over the years our grinding became more purposeful. He was my first kiss, my first taste of another's tongue, and I was his.

And it should have been something meaningful, thinking back, but we were like horny deviant siblings more than boyfriends.

One day our wriggling caused his cock to come out of the side of his loincloth. When he didn't cover up, I cupped his testicles in my hand and rubbed, making him squirm with his eyes closed and his red lips opened wide.

Right after that game my member popped free from the loincloth too. My cousin wasn't forward enough to grope me, so we just continued mashing our pelvises against each other until I had my first squirting orgasm in front of him.

It was a peculiar thing because we were very young. Still, George had seen a cock spit that way before when the adults were playing their own games. Fauns usually seek privacy for sex, but need often outweighs modesty. What Faun child hadn't witnessed two of our people furiously humping in a dark corner of the market? Every teen saw carnal acts enough times to know how to imitate them, which was what George and I were doing.

After our members could no longer be restrained by our clothes, it wasn't long before the game got serious. We became fully naked one day, kissing, groping, and writhing our hot bodies together. My cock pressed against his anus, and, while still not really knowing what I was doing, I pushed the tip of it in.

George winced in pain and we both decided we needed lubricant. I don't remember if I stole it from my step-father or if he got it from his home. The next time we played I worked my organ inside of him, and though he claimed it hurt, he begged me not to stop. We had our first real fuck after a decade of play. His cock erupted with seed as I took him, likely his first orgasm. I came within his snug passage, thrusting as gently as I could.

George could have just as easily been a female as I had no preference. And humans may fear the disastrous ramifications over such play if he were, but faun women are only fertile once a year.

I realized how fertility cycles affected our culture after I came to live with humans. Of course fathers lock away daughters who might get pregnant at any time of the year. For faun women, sex was most often recreation without consequences. If you went to my village, you'd see that the women are equal to the men in expressing their desires.

Once we discovered real sex, we did it five times that day. Sometimes I was inside him, and sometimes he was inside me. That first time, when we were sated to the point of paralysis, I rolled off him not bothering to cover my shiny wet cock. He put his head on my shoulder, leaving his small erection and beautiful blushing ass uncovered. We finally understood. This was what all the fuss was about. We'd unraveled that intimate knowledge we'd been fumbling towards all that time.

And again, I warn the human readers; we were quite some years below the age of marriage. That's the way of my people, because desire rages in our blood as soon as we're old enough for our cocks to get stiff

If fauns are meant to be as chaste as humans are, and I argue that we are not, how would we ever know it?

Consider our decadent schools.

2 Mr. Renherld

My beloved Richard has read my first chapter and laughed with joy. He lauds my talent as an amateur author. I hope I shall continue to live up to his standards. He is most patient, reading of my childhood long before I knew him.

I hope you will be patient as well, dear reader, for my goal is not only to recount the success of the Grand Motley Carnival, or of the stage careers Richard and I had after the carnival's demise, but to acclimate you in depth with the world of the fauns.

Have patience, and I promise you shall learn of the great romance that happened between Richard and I starting in chapter 16.

***

I can't speak for every faun school, I only know of my five room compound in *Schaletar*. If what went on in this facility was unusual, I've had no sign of it.

Playing the way my cousin and I did was forbidden at school where we were supposed to focus on our lessons. When I was in the rooms for the early grades, this was hardly an issue. Trouble started here and there in the middle grades and then became a grand struggle in the final grades.

Once I reached that room which held the last four grades I saw all the boundaries I'd known get broken. When the teacher's back turned, a last-year female student flashed her tit to a boy beside her who gingerly reached over to play with her nipple. A girl near me rubbed her hoof against the ass of the boy in front of her, the boy angling in his seat to

let her hard toes reach under. Two faun girls who had to share a desk would masturbate each other, getting caught when the more buxom of the pair would whimper with orgasm. And I saw that boys could play with one another just as freely, pinching an ass as one walked down the aisle between our desks or exchanging hand jobs before the teacher arrived in the morning. Students hadn't a care if classmates saw their activities, no, in fact they loved to exhibit, and the last-years masturbated openly as they watched.

I'd always heard your world changes when you reach the last room of the school. It had, and marvelously. I felt like an adult now, privy to all the delights proper grown-ups knew. I was keen to participate with either a girl or a boy. The punishments made me hesitate.

Our teacher for the last four years of school was Mr. Renherld, a bachelor aged forty-five. Fauns almost never stay unwed into adulthood because a sexual partner was direly required. For Renherld, teacher of the last-years, a spouse was unnecessary. I learned fast enough he took privileges with the students under the guise of punishment and was never vulnerable to any reprisal.

Renherld was tall, lean, with a sharp nose and chin and with spectacles hiding his cruel eyes. He had the costume of a respectable teacher, the black cap and gown they all wore, but the wicked expressions of his face broadcasted diabolical perversion. He loved his thick wooden paddle, but it was his spindly fingers with bulging joints that most often came against a nubile student's flesh. His black mane of hair made him look sinister, but

also reminded one he was a dandy obsessed with his appearance in his youth.

He'd taught my mother her last years of schooling. Before she died, she spoke of him tenderly, with her eyes glistening. I inherited the man fifteen years removed from her experience. He was still a dandy despite the creases beside his eyes, but one who's cruelty had amplified with age; whose creativity had grown harrowing.

I tell you without exaggeration that this sharpened teacher captivated every student he taught. He had an air of authority which you rarely associated with carnality. In his class we not only saw unrepentant lust from an adult, but were blessed to be the subject of it. He was the first grown-up most fauns in our village had had sex with. It became a rite of passage, common to most all of us, which was why handsome men were always assigned to teach the last-years.

Do I mislead you into thinking him to be a romantic seducer? A gentle initiator of licentious delights? Wipe these notions from your mind. Renherld was a punisher who might have had no intention of granting pleasure. After being subject to his brand of detention you were always sore, and not always sated.

The girl who whimpered her orgasm in the back of the class room had to come to the front. Without being asked, she bent over the teacher's desk, hoisted her skirt up, and pulled her panties down delicately furred legs. My eyes drank in her glorious pale ass and the dewy hair in the crevice below it. I blushed, also, because I didn't yet realize a teacher would condone such exhibition.

Renherld produced his forbidding wooden paddle and squashed both of the girl's plump ass

cheeks beneath a brutal strike. Her yelp made me jolt in my seat.

"One!" the class said in unison.

Renherld spanked again.

"Two!" the class said.

He beat her ass to a glorious pink with five reverberating cracks of the paddle. I could hear the pitiful girl sobbing where she bent over his desk.

After the fifth blow, he clattered down the paddle and rubbed her ass flesh with the knobby fingers of his hand. This made my eyes bulge. He told her to think better of what she'd done and not to misbehave again, all while fondling her. And the girl did nothing but quiver with her thighs and reddened ass cheeks beneath his hand.

Then she was allowed to right her clothes and return to her seat. She stuck her tongue out to one boy in playful defiance to her punishment as she passed.

This was how our school was, dear humans. Nearly mature teenagers forced to expose themselves to the whole class, their bare asses spanked and then groped! For me the punishment was just as sexual as whatever crime we were accused of.

I'm speaking of my first year in this notorious room, and me and the rest my grade were still inhibited. This included George, who no longer played with me. Our games ended soon after we fucked because he was eager to show other older children he was wise to sex. I didn't explore as he did because secrets in my home made me timid beyond my family members. The last time I tried to sleep with George he said he was through playing games with a child.

(This led to a rift between us that lasted until adulthood. Then one day we spoke to each other like old friends in the market and reminisced fondly about our mutual deflowering. These days he's married to a kind wife, has a soldering trade in the workshop of his home, and twin babies.)

George entered the same grade as me and became just as sheepish in the bold new surroundings. We observed, we enjoyed what we saw, but we were the newest class and not brave enough to take part. We hadn't any fear of Renherld as yet because it was said he never initiated the first-years.

I would quickly learn this was no longer true.

3 The Bully

I finished an exam early and was allowed to go outside to the water pump for a drink. A senior boy followed me and pulled my tail. I looked at him, not defensive, because the tug of a tail wasn't seen as aggressive.

"So you're Madio's son, is that right? Kali?" said the older student, who was taller than me and already filled with the muscles of a man. I tried to hide the desire in my eyes as I met his gaze.

"Yep," I said, despite actually being sired by someone else. Madio was the stepfather who reared me after my mother's death. I wiped my mouth with forced nonchalance.

"I bet you've had a man inside you." He had a sideways smile when he said it.

I smiled with embarrassment in return. "Sure I have."

"Know why I know?"

I shook my head.

He leaned close to my face, making me feel threatened. "Because your mom's dead, and your dad never got a new one, never goes out to the town. He stays up in that big house of yours doing nothing."

I became confused.

"Pretty thing that you are, Kali, I bet you're who he's fucking to get by."

I scoffed with my heart racing.

He grabbed me by my arm. "Oh, come on. Admit it."

"You don't know shit!"

He turned away with an angry grin. At this point he might have punched me. I was hoping he really meant it when he called me pretty. Our kind often channeled our anger into sex.

He licked his lip, giving me a sign things wouldn't veer toward violence. "I don't care if you admit it or not. If your ass is broken in, then you'll handle my dick easy. None of the other boys'll take it cause they say it's too big."

I almost went dizzy with how much blood rushed to my cock. Even if he was an asshole, he was a gorgeous asshole. I was already craving the strength of his large arms around my body. And I couldn't help myself. I reached out and cupped his groin.

The boy opened his legs and let me get a feel. Yes, he was huge. Long and thick, with a hot cap that pulsed through the fabric of his loincloth. I nudged the tip out of the side of his garment and wet my finger on his slit.

When I looked up at him my eyes had to be shining. "I can take it."

The confirmation made him grab me and give me a kiss. His body was hard and hot enough to warm me through our clothes. He got his tongue between my lips and worked my mouth with smoldering skill. I felt a tingling rush over my skin, my legs growing weak, my head getting dizzy. This was the first time I felt the surge of energy someone passionate could cause me. It was hollow of any tender emotion, but still thrilling.

But another teacher caught us and reported us to Renherld. It was time for school to let out. He yelled in front of the class that we would both have our bare asses spanked on Monday.

"And you, first-year," Renherld said with a suspicious grin, "you'll get the worst of it!"

The older boy didn't care. Me? I was horrified and aroused. My nipples perked under the sheer white tunic I wore making chafing peaks as I walked.

Besides having us fret all weekend, Mr. Renherld gave us write-up slips to take home before we left. Whenever you were punished at school, you had to inform your parent and get them to sign off on a slip. This way you'd be punished twice for the same crime.

I didn't mind this part. My step-father was exactly what the older boy described: he never remarried after my mother's death, never went to town, and had no occupation. He stayed in the large home which belonged to my grandparents living meagerly off an inheritance.

I knew it would please him to have an excuse to punish me.

4 Step-Father

I mentioned before I was not as bold as my cousin George. There were several things in my youth which caused me to withdraw as much as one with an overpowering sex drive could.

First, my birth father died when I was four. Mother said he drank poisonous ale, but her mother, my grandmother, said he drank so much and so often that he pickled his body from the inside, killing himself. The truth was somewhere in between and came from the retired owner of the tavern where his body had been found.

My father drank whiskey, not ale, and he was drunk so often my mother had to expel him from our home. His own family had long since disowned him, so he slept behind one of the two taverns in our village. He was found dead with an empty whiskey jug hooked to his thumb. Either the whiskey or exposure ended him that night. My mother did not shed a tear for him and bade me to do the same.

I didn't cry because I did not know him, only his absence and the pain that would form in my mother's face when I asked why I didn't have a father to take me tuber hunting or mountain climbing. The only memory I have of my father was of him standing at our doorway asking my mother for money. He tussled my hair when I came to the door. I remember wondering who this man was to be touching me in such a familiar way. I hoped he was not my father because he stunk of urine.

The man who represented father to me came into my life a year after my birth father's death. Madio had no vices and was a dedicated laborer. I know not why my grandmother despised him. She claimed he was uneducated, but Madio could build a porch or a bridge over a gully with just a felled tree a pile of metal tools. How could someone with such skill be stupid?

Mother said the real reason grandmother hated him was because he was a satyr and not a faun. I hadn't the ability to tell the difference at that age. He was just a kind, caring man who adored me enough to adopt me and give me his name, Hartswit. Because of that adoption I use both the words father and step-father to describe him.

Mother was nearly ten years older than Madio, who had remained unwed into his early thirties. He came from an eastern country considered more primitive than ours for the opportunities in Schaletar, and worked as laborer on the grounds of my grandparent's mansion. His trysts with mother were ignored by her parents since he was rugged and irresistible to young men and women alike. To my mother though, he was light in her eyes, and she was intelligent beauty he'd dreamed to partner with.

She convinced him to mate with her when she was in heat to force her parents to allow them to marry. The scheme worked, but he never received their approval. My grandfather accused him of marrying mother for her riches. I knew it wasn't true, and I felt it proven after her death. My father became a broken man, existing only because he had to rear me. He did so in a deep gloom.

Mother had become pregnant by him at forty-one. Friends and family congratulated her while whispering the child was bound to miscarry.

It did not, but both she and the baby died.

With my mother dead my grandparents cursed my step-father openly. They blamed her death on him since he was of a different breed and considered too beastly to mate with their kind. I saw how much these accusations wounded him when he was already devastated by the loss of his beloved.

Their cruelty was the reason I refused to let them take me. I stayed with the man my mother had loved with all her heart, and by doing so forced my grandparents to let him keep our house, which was legally their property.

My new father had done nothing but adore my mother. He deserved no ire when he suffered her loss greater than anyone. I was proud to be his solace during this time of tremendous suffering, and yet my grandparents refused to visit me due to my betrayal.

Madio wouldn't leave our house after mother's death. I ventured out very little as well. I had to attend school which was a two mile walk, so I also did all the shopping. Father would say we needed oats or wool grease and then dig up coins from a deep basket. Along I went. Everyone in the market knew of me and my cloistered step-father, who was still ravishing in appearance, but tainted with controversy and grief. They said nothing about him, but I noticed the examination of their eyes. Some of them wondered if my father might be cajoled out for some play. I avoided their inquiries since he would never step past the front door of our home.

During that short period when George and I discovered proper sex, and engaged in it daily, my step-father said my scent had changed. I thought it was from my discharge, but that began years before I fucked George. He said I was more like a man now. I agreed. I was proud that someone as rugged as my step-father recognized the carnal change within me. Perhaps I'd be just like him soon.

I must mention that my mother had been a great collector when she was alive, and many vases, statuettes, lamps, and decorated plates stood on shelves throughout our parlor. Madio had me dust these weekly, and I did so without complaint because I was eager to please him. However, I was still a teenager, and one day while running through the house I knocked down a white vase with pink flowers and a golden lip.

It broke neatly into two pieces. I gathered them and brought them to my father hoping we could glue it. He was having a period of brooding where he'd stay in his bed and speak little. This happened often enough for it not to concern me. I knew he'd eventually exit his room, chatty and playful, catching me for a bout of wrestling. Still, I had to bother his present gloom for the sake of mother's vase.

"Can we glue this vase back together, you think?"

His eyes were on it, but he didn't seem to see. I wondered if he'd even heard me. Then he sat up, shirtless and still with a fine definition of muscle, to furrow his brows.

"What happened?"

"Oh, I knocked it over."

"You knocked it over? How?"

"I was running." I said it earnestly because my step-father had never been a cruel man. Distraught and reclusive to the world, but doting and rambunctious to me when he was out of his brooding.

He took the fragments in his hand. "This was a very important piece from your mother's collection."

That made me feel guilty. "Can't we glue it back together?"

He considered a while. "We'll try, snowy." He looked at me while saying my nickname; my hair and skin were as white as mother's had been. His brown eyes held a glimmer. "But I must punish you."

"Oh," I said, with a defiant brow. When had my father punished me before? I couldn't even remember the last time he'd shouted. "How are you going to punish me?"

He drew back his covers and stood. "With a good hard beating, I'm afraid."

I scoffed. Surely I was too old for such a thing. "Oh."

He placed a strong but gentle hand on my shoulder. "First, I'll have a bath, though. You go downstairs and prepare supper."

I nodded and hurried to obey. That he'd gotten out of bed and was even taking a bath made me joyful. It looked like I'd jolted him out of his brooding phase, and all I'd have to do was get a beating. It wouldn't be too terrible. I trusted my step-father.

I made potato cakes with sprigs of herbs. Father came down with his beard in a wet ringlet wearing only his loincloth. The full view of his body always impressed me. What man in the

village wouldn't want legs as thick and hooves as broad as he? His abdomen was long with round muscles trailing to a crotch whose curls of black hair couldn't stay inside his garment.

He sniffed the air with a grin. "Smells good. You got your mom's cooking skills in addition to her looks."

I scoffed with a smile this time. He was definitely out of his depression, which made me giddy. I served us and we chattered on about school and what he'd read in our village tribune. I didn't think about the threat of punishment. Everything felt easy and right between us. These were the days I loved best.

After I cleared the table, he wiped his mouth and stood. "All right. Let's get on with reddening that fine white ass of yours."

Now, I might have complained my way out of the punishment. My step-father was kind, and I didn't feel as though he truly wanted to punish me. But his language made me curious. Would he really hit me? He'd never done that before. Would he hug me afterwards and tell me he loved me? He had done that, but not for years. I would do most anything for such affection.

"Right. Let's go up stairs."

I followed him feeling uneasiness mingled with intrigue. He brought me to his bedroom. There was a clean sheet now covering his bed.

My father snuffled as though trying to hide his nervousness. "Bend over the side of the bed and pull down your loincloth."

I didn't move at once. My face felt like it got hot from a blush. We never shared our nakedness with each other. Now he wanted me to show him my ass?

He nudged his chin. "Go on. No sense stalling."

I went to the bed still hesitant and then untied the loop of cloth that went over my short tail. My loincloth went slack. I pulled it down, feeling a tickle on the skin of my ass cheeks as they were exposed.

"Lovely." I could tell my father was talking through a smile. "All right. Bend over then."

Bending over made all my skin tingle. Now my naked ass was jutting out for him to see every bit of it. I stared at the white wall in front of me not knowing what to feel.

My father moved beside me and clasped my tail with one hand. With the other he gave me a smack on the bottom. I grew even more confused. It didn't hurt much, and it seemed stupid to go through all this ceremony for what was just a pantomime of a real punishment.

He cleared his throat and smacked my other side, again getting no reaction from me. His hand slapped the first side again, making me sting slightly, then the other side. He continued softly swatting alternating cheeks for several minutes.

Just as my ass was growing warm he spoke in a deep throaty voice that was unlike him. "Bad, bad, boy. That was your mother's favorite vase."

My voice was without any heaviness. "I thought she loved the blue and red one best."

"Are you talking back?"

"No. I thought—"

"I see the spanking's not getting through to you." His voice was insincere. "What if I was to do something even worse? Would that get through to you?" He poked his finger against my asshole.

I gave a gasp that felt like it came out of my entire body.

With a sudden jerk he stomped away from me. His voice grew choked. "Never mind." He began shouting. "It's fine! Your punishment's over!"

"Dad!"

He halted in the doorway. In the seconds he stood there I got my thoughts together. I figured out what the punishment was about. I realized why he was rushing away in shame. What I didn't know was what I felt about it. I couldn't find my feelings fast enough to decide what to say, but didn't want him to fall back into his depression. Couldn't I endure what he wanted to stop that?

"Dad," I said again, softly this time, "you can finish punishing me."

He looked back and his flushed face confirmed my suspicions. His eyes were large and shiny. His lower lip trembled. I was bent over his bed with my ass exposed and I knew he was filled with desire for me. It tormented him if not for a long while then at least at that moment. He'd attempted to resist, and yet, such an elaborate ruse as this made me sure it had been in his thoughts.

"Finish punishing me." I swallowed. "I'm not scared of you."

He rushed back and dropped to his knees behind me. His hands roved over my buttocks.

"Oh, my darling boy. Why did you become so beautiful?"

I was sensitive and his caresses to my spanked bottom felt good. My eyes closed. I rested my head on his bed and let the forbidden happen.

"You fucked George, didn't you?"

"Mm-hm."

"Did he fuck you too? Put it all the way in?"

"A long time ago."

"So you're not too young anymore."

His thumb pressed against my asshole. I let out a nasal sound of pleasure. Such a tender place—back then I was stunned by how good it felt to be touched there. My hoof bent up off the floor.

"Don't hurt me," I said. My voice was quiet and my eyes were still closed.

He moistened a finger and rubbed my anus. My eyes rolled back beneath my eyelids. I felt my hardening cock fighting for space under my stomach.

"I won't hurt you, Kali." I'm glad he used my name instead of the nickname of my childhood. He was whispering as though someone might hear us. "If it hurts, tell me to stop. If it feels wrong, tell me to stop. Don't cry—make me stop before you feel like crying, or I don't know what I'll do."

"I don't feel like crying." I wasn't whispering, but my voice was soft.

He buried his face in my cheeks and licked my hole. His tongue lapped hard and fast making both my legs swing up from the floor. I moaned with my mouth open wide. That sensitive place was barraged by hot wet buds, shooting potent pleasure throughout my groin, making me forget the truth of what was happening. I was caught in the thrall of incredible ecstasy.

My arms thrashed on the bed. "That feels so good!"

"Like it?" He pushed the tip of a finger in me without causing pain. My ring throbbed around it. "You'll make some boy very happy." He wriggled the finger, and I stuttered my moans. "But

those noises you make, that squirming, the way your ass cheeks tremble—what am I to do, Kali? You're even sweeter than I dreamed of."

"You dreamed of this?" I said, breathless.

He kissed one mound of my ass. "You've grown into your mother. I miss her so badly. Her white skin. Everyone else is disgusting. She was perfection. Her mind. Her body." His finger got all the way inside me. I whimpered and writhed against the mattress. "You're perfection also, my boy."

The pleasure made me go desperate. "But what are you going to do?"

His hand withdrew from my ass, leaving only the throbbing of my tight hole. He stood and took a canister from the dresser beside us.

"I won't hurt you." He slathered wool grease between my legs, nudging my testicles as he coated me. "If it hurts tell me to stop. Promise me."

"Uh-huh."

I opened my thighs to allow him access. He reached up and palmed my testicles. The sublime hot touch made my cock leak dew on the bed. I let out a long throaty moan while angling my hips to press myself into his hand.

"You're so sweet, Kali. Stay this way. Don't have regret. Don't hate me."

I was unsure, but said, "I won't."

He pushed my thighs back together. I felt the tip of his cock pressing between them, just below my ass. His organ worked between my oiled thighs and bumped the back of testicles. He took a firm grasp of my sides.

"Is that good?" he said.

"Just my legs?"

"Yes." He thrust. His cock picked up my tender sack with every push inward. "But I want your ass. I need it. Unless you make me stop, I'm going to fuck you there. No now. Eventually."

His wet tip mashing my balls robbed my focus from his words. I moaned and ground my cock against the bed.

His finger, still greased, pushed into my asshole. My cries went up an octave. I wiggled my ass to feel him move against my ring.

"Start opening yourself for me. Stretch this ring." His thumb pinched against his finger to indicate the strong band of muscle. "Put things inside yourself covered in grease."

I gasped. His cock jabbed the bulge behind my testicles and gave me a shock of ecstasy.

"When you can fit three fingers inside, I'm going to fuck you."

His throaty voice was so far removed from what I knew of him. It caused flutters in my middle.

"And you'll like it, I can tell. You'll beg for it!"

He gave a final hard thrust and ejaculated between my legs. His body closed over mine, squeezing me as his cock spasmed. His grunts filled my ears.

I loved this part of what had happened most of all, the way he held me.

His breaths stilled on my back. He peeled himself off and turned me around. My hard cock was there for him to see, gleaming and dark red at the moist tip.

He met my eyes. "Can I touch it?"

I was gasping. "It's sensitive."

"Stop fussing and let me do this."

I used sex as a method to pull him from his periods of brooding. Most other times he would announce I was due a punishment and I would surrender to his bed. Without tears. Without sickness or dread. I pretended what we did was normal.

Good or ill, this practice sated me. I didn't seek sex outside our home, because it was too pleasurable there, and again, I feared growing close to anyone. I'd had only two lovers in my life by the time I reached Renherld's classroom: cousin and father.

Sometimes I'd catch the latter weeping and vowing to never touch me again. He'd call himself despicable.

I had no strong emotions for our peculiar activity. He wasn't really my father. It was impossible to serve him how I wished to if I tried to fathom some wrongness. The older I grew the less I saw him as dad.

"It's made you stop brooding," I said to him a year after we began having sex. "If no one finds out then what's the harm? We can be normal father and son except for when we're in bed."

"How can you have so little care over what I do to you?"

I refused to meet his tearful eyes. If I hated it, I would make it stop, and then I'd have to run away from him. I worried I'd see things this way and ruin everything we had. I wished not to consult my pathos or that of a step-father I still loved.

It was best to let what happened happen.

5 School Punishment

"Do you fancy this boy they caught you kissing?" my step-father asked when I showed him my punishment slip over supper.

"No, he's a cretin." I took another bite of my vegetable stew. "But I might want a little fun with him. He's good-looking enough for that."

My father grunted and gave a nod. I feared he might see this boy as a rival and this would trouble me. We could not be a true coupling. I'd thought that fact understood.

"Have your fun with him, but not at school," father said.

"Could I bring him back here?"

"I suppose. But be discreet. A father oughtn't to have any business in his son's sex-life."

He spoke of what a normal father ought or ought not to do, not about us. I understood this with sharp clarity—and I was grateful. We need not be anymore abnormal than we already were.

He put aside his dish and folded his strong hands together. "Do you want me to punish you for this?"

My lips parted. He'd never asked before. The presence of a new figure made him cautious. He accepted I might one day leave him for something that was wholesome. In that moment he gave me a choice.

"Beat me rotten," I said with a small smile. He'd granted me some liberty, and I repaid him with the reminder that I was, for now, still his possession.

Father laughed quietly and rose to lead me upstairs. We had an energetic fuck. My long body twisted into the right position for him to pierce my sweet spot, which he did with a fury he knew my limber form could withstand.

I describe this to you because I never abhorred the sex. It seemed my flesh was incapable of disliking it. I cared not for the danger of it, but I was enchanted. I will always admit this. To say different would be a lie against the memory of my step-father. I still loved him when he died.

That was some years later though.

In the present of that time I had to accept my real punishment at school. As I made my two mile trek Monday morning, Cretin, as we will call him, caught up to walk beside me.

"Ready for your whipping?" he said with a toothy smile. I understood his nature was that of a bully, but one who wanted to fuck me badly enough not to be violent.

"Not really," I said. "Have you been spanked before?"

"Of course. I'm a fourth-year. I've gotten my ass beaten a good two dozen times. So will you when you reach my grade."

I groaned. "I'd sooner drop-out."

This made him erupt in laughter.

"It's the humiliation. I don't want the whole class to see my bare bottom."

"It would be humiliating," Cretin said, "if it didn't happen to all of us, over and over again, all the time."

This was true enough. I'd seen most of third and fourth-years expose themselves for a beating already.

"You won't be spanked in front of the class, though."

I looked at him.

"He's going to give you a detention. You mark my words."

"Why? He said he would spank us."

Cretin blocked me on the cobble walk. He leaned down with a menacing grin. "Cause he knows what I know, Kali. Your ass's been broken in by a grown man already. There won't be no harm in him fucking you. That's exactly what he's going to do."

"He doesn't fuck the first-years." I'd become defensive.

Cretin licked his lips. "But he'll fuck you. Just watch."

He trotted off then, and I had to follow. We didn't dare arrive after the first bell.

Renherld began his lesson right after the bell, writing chalk notes on his blackboard while lecturing with his back to us. Cretin and I exchanged confused glances. Had he forgotten about our punishments?

"The butterfly will lay its eggs on the underside of the leaf its species eat," Renherld said, while scrawling a bullet list of the butterfly's life-cycle. "Once born the caterpillars will gorge on leaves, growing rapidly. Their skin can't stretch, so they must molt several times before reaching full size." He turned and his voice rose to a virulent shout. "Much the way Pruitt's ass will molt after I've given him his beating. Get up here and take your punishment!"

Cretin (we'll call him Pruitt now) scrapped back the legs of his chair and dragged himself to the front. I sat with my stomach roiling and my spit

going cold as each sharp strike of the paddle landed on his bare ass. Renherld didn't bother to fondle him afterwards, but instead pointed a knobby finger at me.

"As for you, Kali, spanking's too good for such a disobedient first-year. I'll see to you after class in detention."

Pruitt snorted a laugh at me as he passed to return to his seat. "Told you."

A humiliating beating would have almost been preferable to stewing in my terror all class. How could mother have been so enchanted with this vicious man?

I gathered that he intended to punish me with sex. This would be a far cry from the gentle lovemaking I had with my step-father. I trusted that man, and could therefore share my body without apprehension.

Renherld was a pervert which delighted the older grades, but frightened my doe-eyes. Sex for fun was lovely, sex with someone I cared for, even a step-father, could be comforting, but sex for punishment? The concept sickened me.

That was because I had no comprehension.

When the final bell rang, I trembled in my seat as the rest of the class galloped out. Renherld marked papers for a few minutes without looking at me. My stomach remained in knots. Again I wondered if he'd forgotten he gave me detention, or if he even knew I was there.

Outside the door was the small corridor that connected the five rooms of the school house. Students were tromping by with loud hooves, hollering to each other, rustling through their baskets for book bags or what have you. Through it

all, Renherld kept his head lowered and his pen focused on the papers he graded.

Another teacher named Mrs. Franc popped her head into the doorway. "Will you be going to the lottery?" she asked, with one slender hand curling around the side jamb. Three numbers were drawn daily and four numbers weekly for lotteries in the city square each weekday.

Renherld gestured to me. "Afraid not."

Mrs. Franc, having been my middle grade teacher, gave me a scathing glare. "Why Kali, how can you be in trouble so early in the school year? For shame."

I conjured my most pathetic expression and said, "I'm sorry." Fear dripped from my voice that cracked her chiding demeanor.

She looked back at Renherld. "Well now, you won't be too hard on him will you?"

"Tut, tut, my dear Cadence. Lessons must be learned early and learned well. Particularly for boys who flout the rules in the very first quarter."

She shrugged and turned to go. "You do what you see best, of course." My last hope for mercy sauntered away. I was crestfallen.

Renherld addressed me once she left. "Open your literature book and copy lines from Du'carte."

I quickly dragged out the book to obey. I'd write a thousand lines if he wished. This was the punishment I hoped for.

Alas, it was just his way of buying time. I wrote lines until the sports team finished practice in the field, and students doing after school studies finished their lessons. Renherld was keeping me busy until the building was good and truly empty.

When there was nary a sound he exited to the corridor to check each room. My heart now

raced. What diabolical plot did he need such solitude to unfold?

He returned and closed the classroom door, securing the latch to lock it. Next he closed the blinds on all three windows. It grew so dark a gas lamp had to be lit for us to see each other. His face became even more harrowing in the dramatic shadows of the thin light.

"Enough writing. Get up here. Now!"

I obeyed with my head down and my arms hugged close to my chest.

"Oh what is this?" Renherld said while peeling my arms from my body. "Feeling sorry for yourself? Perhaps you'll think better next time before engaging in debauchery on school grounds!"

Wasn't that what he was about to do? I didn't dare say it.

He spun me around and had me bend over his desk with my ass facing him. The rough hand he used to pull off my loincloth made me fret that he'd tear it. Then I endured noxious visions of walking home bare-assed and victimized by every faun who saw me. Fortunately he stripped me without ripping the cotton of my garment. He pulled my cloth to the floor and then commanded me to step out of it.

"Spread your hooves! Arch your back!"

I obeyed the sharp commands hoping my compliance would earn me some mercy. He clasped my short tail in one hand and beat my buttocks with the other, switching from side to side as father once did. The strikes echoed with harsh slapping sounds, but I knew this spanking was gentler than his paddle. I accepted the beating with a clenched jaw, hugging the rim of his desk as I gave full access to my naked bottom.

Again, this was a punishment I could endure: a private spanking away from the eyes of my classmates. I would have thanked my wicked teacher if this were truly all he meant for me to suffer.

He ceased beating me when my ass was stinging and hot. I felt the bulbous bones of his knuckles as he caressed my buttocks, kneading the flesh close to my crease.

"How obedient you are now. I might not believe you committed any crime in our yard." He cupped my testicles, making me gasp at the shock of lurid sensation. "But I know better."

He continued with his spanking, this time beating both throbbing cheeks of my ass for twice as long as before. I grunted with my pain. He burned my flesh raw.

My nipples hard and my cock strangely erect, I continued to make my body prostrate to his beating. Grunts turned to whimpers, and then sobs. Finally he ceased and rubbed my scalded buttocks once more.

"You're tolerant, aren't you? Quietly sobbing rather than showing disobedience. I might have respect for you, were you not so willful." He massaged me with both hands, his thumbs breaching my sensitive crease. My eyes rolled back in my head apparently with pleasure. I didn't understand how that was possible.

"I'm sorry, Mr. Renherld," I said, breathless. My motives were unclear as I spoke, but the eroticism in my voice gave me a cue. A fuck would be better than more spanking. I was enticing him— perhaps I was even eager for him. Delirium from my beating so beset me I was unsure.

"Are you sorry?" Renherld said. "You were incredibly naughty. It's quite an affront to me, you realize."

"I didn't mean to offend you." Now that I knew my goal I became fully entranced by it.

Fuck me, you insidious pervert. Take what you want so you'll stop beating me.

"Well what are we to do about this, Kali?" he said, still stroking my ass. "Spanking is hardly a fit punishment."

Ugh. Get on with it you simpering perv.

"If you would show me leniency," I said, "I would endure most any punishment."

"Is that so?"

One of his hands removed from my ass. I saw him open a desk drawer. His other hand came off my flesh, and he unscrewed a jar of lubricant. The cold goo was slathered between my cheeks onto my asshole. Renherld massaged the grease against my bud with both hard thumbs, making continuos downward sweeps. I gasped and rose onto the tips of my hooves. The stimulation made my cock swell to my navel.

"What shall we do, young Kali? What shall we do?" He continued greasing my asshole with thumbs that pressed my ring inward. A moan became choked in my throat. My ass cheeks trembled around his hands. It was such exquisite ecstasy. This wicked teacher knew precisely how to pleasure me.

"Do whatever would please you," I said, still with only half a voice. My thighs and calves strained beneath his rapturous onslaught.

"It would please me to punish you," he said, "and I think I know just the way."

He tossed his cap and gown. I saw them cumulate on the floor beside me. Then I heard the zipper of his pants.

"You're not going to make a fuss, are you, first-year?"

My brow twitched.

"Parents are most unwelcome in my classroom. You'll suffer dearly if you sic your father on me. I assure you of this. I have leave to punish my students in whatever manner I wish."

His words reassured me. I assumed he fucked students indiscriminately. Apparently, there were limits to his power.

"Punish me," I said softly. "I won't complain." I felt it better to get fucked in private rather than spanked in public. Perhaps my compliance would spare me future humiliation?

His greased cock perked against my anus. "You sure now, first year? Don't be a wretch. I abhor wretches."

I closed my eyes and braced myself while my body pressed against his desk.

"Fuck me."

He pushed the head of his cock past my ring and I let out a moan of ecstasy. His organ was fatter than father's, but my ass was so well-trained it caused me no pain.

Renherld furthered his length into me by slow degrees. His pelvis connected to the reddened cheeks of my ass.

"My, my," he said, "Experienced aren't you?"

I responded with a lengthy moan and a buck of my hips against his groin. *Shut up and get on with it.*

Renherld clutched my sides and pounded into me like a faun who hadn't had sex for months. Which might have been true as summer break had finished recently, and I was his first detention. His girth stretched my insides in a sublimely pleasurable way. I could not resist the soft moans that came forth with his every inward plunge, and my cock bristled with need for an orgasm.

These lurid details may offend those of gentle sensibilities. I only wish it made clear I enjoyed what was happening.

In less than a minute he gushed a flood of hot seed inside of me. This was when I saw the true Renherld, for he moaned and hugged his body against his back.

He pulled out of me, wiping the issuance that came forth with a handkerchief. I lifted myself from his desk and partway turned. I expected to dress and leave. A rough hand to my shoulder turned me around and then urged me to perch on the edge of his desk. My punishment was not yet over.

Renherld looked at my stiff ruddy cock, and I felt my cheeks get hot with embarrassment. Such exposure in such a forbidden setting made me cringe bodily. Inside, however, I was overcome by the eroticism. My strict teacher was licking his lips at the sight of my arousal.

"It seems that wasn't punishment for you at all." He slapped my erection with one flippant hand, making my naked ass bounce on his desk. "You think I mean to pleasure you, first-year? Deviant lascivious boy!"

I was the deviant one? The words did not resonate in the least. I was but an accommodating teen before a vile pervert. His words sounded more like a performance than the truth.

"Take off your tunic!"

I lifted my shirt over my head to obey. It was tossed aside near the pile of his own garments. My pink nipples hardened once exposed to the air and Renherld's eager gaze.

"Now clasp the back of your horns with both hands."

I did so.

"Keep your hands there, boy. Grip those horns tight. And don't you dare lower your hands to divert me. Do that and you'll suffer thrice the punishment I intended."

I blinked at him, fully nude, my ass cheeks connected to his desk, and my elbows pointed upwards as I gripped my horns.

Renherld took a ruler out of a desk drawer. Before I could try to fathom what he meant to do, he used it to swat the underside of my cock. I yelped with my chest jolting. The sharp sting was all the more potent for the sensitive place it struck.

"Naughty boy," he said, pelting my erection with the flat of his ruler once more. "Look at this!"

He gave a swat to my red helmet, which had emerged from its sheath of foreskin. My teeth and eyes clenched at the exhilarating shock of pain. At the same time a dribble of clear issuance exited my slit to drip down the length of my organ.

"Filthy! Filthy!" He took a clean handkerchief and squeezed my cock to erase the liquid.

I gasped harder than I had during his strikes. His strong fist built the pressure of orgasm right at my tender base.

"Urgh! I think I'm going to…"

"You better not you disgusting wretch!"

He folded back the wooden ruler above my nipple and let it crack free. I screamed. My hard nubbin seared through a rush of pain followed by a delicious pulsation. I was so entranced by the sensation I didn't realize he held the ruler to give a matching blow to the other side. I screamed again and my chest heaved with my panting breaths.

"Open your legs wider!"

I obeyed. He patted the ruler against my testicles, making me contort my face in anticipation.

"You climax without my leave and I'll beat your sacks. You want that?"

Desperate words came up. "No, sir. Please, no."

"Right." He moved the ruler away from my most delicate place. "Take your beating without defiance."

"Yes, sir."

He whipped the underside of my shaft with the ruler. I sniveled with my jaw falling wide.

"Perhaps if you're good, I'll reward you."

Another lighting hot pelt landed on my shaft. I let my tears free. My organ throbbed so virulently with heat you could see its twitching movement. I watched it, awaiting the next strike with wet eyes. Renherld set down the ruler and coated his hand with grease.

"Don't orgasm." He gripped the bottom of my cock and inched his hand up, squeezing every deep fiber of my swollen cock as he did.

My breaths became desperate. I hadn't known how close I was until he touched me. The beating had been foreplay to me. Imagine—pain intensifying arousal. I realized I enjoyed the fear and illicit pain. It was like an intoxicating weed.

And now it made obeying my teacher's order nearly impossible.

"Please stop please! I'm going to come!"

He released me in the nick of time. My shaft stood as firmly as it had when his hand braced it.

Renherld snatched the ruler and gave me three strikes in a second. Both my nipples renewed their blaze, and the helmet of my cock received another vicious crack. I screamed and my body curled forward with my sobs.

"You filthy disgusting wretch! I barely finished a stroke! Are you so polluted you take pleasure in this?"

I now quivered as I wept.

"Well? Answer me!"

"I like it," I heard myself say. "Only not on the cap, please sir."

Renherld looked at me with his expression of disdain for a moment, then his face transmogrified into a horrifying smile. He brought his knobby fingers to my testicles and massaged me in a way he had to know was pleasing.

"Oh you like it, do you? And you'll even admit it. My, my." His eyes moved from my face to my cock. "What a special boy you are."

With that he engulfed my cock in his mouth. I kept hold of my horns, flabbergasted. Renherld sucked with hollow cheeks pulling my member with enough strength to nudge my pelvis. I could only enjoy this for a single pass before panic struck me.

"Sir, oh sir! I'm going to come!"

He let my cock pop free from his lips. Eyes that now sparkled looked up at me.

"If you come in my mouth, I'll give you the worst spanking I've ever given any student in my career. You'll not be able to sit for a month."

My eyes bulged in horror. Even worse, he resumed his vigorous blowjob, tugging my organ with his suction and bobbing his head.

"Sir! No! I can't hold back!" I sobbed while squirming with my buttocks on the desks. "Stop! Please!" For harrowing seconds I maintained my control, but his tight gliding mouth defeated me. "Oh please—I can't...!"

My testicles clenched upwards and seed gushed from my sensitized slit. It had to be the most powerful orgasm of my life. My stomach muscles squeezed with each rapturous spasm. Renherld was still sucking, coaxing the juice of my manhood. I finished with a whimper, my tender cock still in an aggressive vise.

"Stop!"

Renherld let the organ pop free from his lips again, making my abused helmet twinge with over stimulation. He ran his clenched fist from the base to the top of my cock as I wailed with a sob. A final drop of opaque white seed was pushed from my slit. Renherld licked it.

He sat on his desk chair and opened his pants. I saw the oddly crooked cock that had impaled my asshole minutes before. Renherld poured lubricant on it and plumped it with several strokes of his hand.

"Turn around and sit on my lap," he said with a jerk of his chin. "Get it up inside you."

I swallowed with difficulty, my throat still raw from my sobs, and positioned his cock with my hand so I could sit on it. I had momentarily removed my hand from my horn, but was not

scolded. The grease and the way he'd primed me before allowed me to take him into my anus without difficulty. I sat on his lap with his organ deep inside me.

Renherld clutched me around the stomach. "Open your legs so the back of your thighs are braced on the armrests."

I did so, swerving my hips and maneuvering my legs while still impaled. Bracing on the armrests granted me some lift off his cock. Only half his member remained inside.

"Good." He reached up and rubbed hard circles over my nipples.

I hummed a moan at the pleasure. My cock had drooped, but was still thickened. The pinpointed stimulation made it rise.

"Now for your spanking."

He tilted back the chair and grasped my hips. His cock jabbed upwards into me, filling my insides in a spec of a second. He pummeled upwards, making my ass slap against his groin. I bounced haplessly, the ring of my ass pulsing from the furious onslaught.

"Yes!" I sang the word like a moan. He fucked me so virulently my member flailed and banged against my stomach.

Renherld paused, gasping while I enjoyed the after effects of his rapid fuck. Without thinking my hand went to my cock and gently stroked. I didn't intend to masturbate to orgasm. I felt myself absently, letting my hand add to the pleasure I felt in my ass.

"What are you doing, naughty boy?"

"It felt so good," I said, drunk with euphoria on top of him.

"Naughty, naughty boy." He rubbed my nipples again, and I cooed. My hand grew more purposeful.

I was naughty. Other students would be demure and embarrassed through such a punishment. They'd like it, but not with the abandon I showed. It was my step-father's initiation of me. He'd taught me to enjoy sex. I couldn't resist but to revel in my pleasure when someone fucked me right.

"I think we might need more detentions. You make no effort to learn your lessons."

How could I take him in earnest when he rubbed my nipples and had his cock wedged in my ass? I assumed this was his way of asking me to approve a diabolical courtship.

"You can do whatever you wish to me, as often as you please," I said, now arching my pelvis to work his cock in and out of me. "Only, please, sir. Don't ever spank me in front of the class. I can't bear the humiliation."

"You underestimate yourself."

I turned the top half of my body back to pout at him. "Please," I whispered. "Wouldn't you rather punish me in private?"

Renherld's lower lip quivered. He grasped the back of my head and joined our mouths in a kiss. I opened my jaw for him, meeting his slick tongue with my own. Seducing him would spare me the noxious punishment I abhorred. I'd discovered my sexual powers in that moment.

Renherld broke from my lips and I saw him swallow. "We shall see," he said, but I was certain I'd have my way. I smiled sensuously at him to add a final bit of enticement.

Renherld clutched my hips once more. "Oh, you are trouble boy. I can see that already."

Once again he pummeled his cock upwards inside me. I let my moans ring through the classroom. I wanted him to long for my body again after this. My hand continued yanking on my member until a thinner spray of seed erupted. I gave high pitch cries to alert him to my orgasm. This set off Renherld, who jabbed his cock deep and granted me the luxurious feeling of hot liquid gushing inside me.

After that, we separated and cleaned up. My limp organ twinged as I stuffed it in my loincloth.

Renherld and I parted outside without speaking to each other. It was fine. I needed no tenderness or reassurance. Renherld was the one who needed these things from me. So long as I obliged him I was certain to receive the special treatment I required.

And I know, dear readers, you find me obscene, but I ask you, if you lived in a land where teachers took liberties with their students would it not be best to enjoy such a thing rather than to descend into shame and despair? This was truly the way of the realm I grew up in. My tolerance was a gift, not a point of humiliation.

6 First Year

Renherld never spanked me in front of the class. In my first year I found this to be both a blessing and a curse. As you know, I was a most withdrawn student, and thus regarded as mysterious by my peers. That trait became amplified once they realized they would never get to view my naked ass and the bulge of my testicles between my thighs. This made those in the higher grades desire me.

I capitalized with some of the more gregarious older girls. I loved their full breasts and uninhibited wantonness. A good dozen times I brought a nearly grown girl-faun home and hid away with her in my bedroom under the guise of studying.

The jewel of our class, the gorgeous Babbette had detentions with Renherld just as often as I. At the start of our 'study session' she threw me on my bed, pulled my cock out of my loincloth, and rode me to shivering climax. It was only once she was sated that I could roll us over and get her enormous breasts out of her dress. I humped that horny girl as ruggedly as Renherld had me.

Will any human blame me for accepting these girls' advances? I was well enough endowed for my age to excite them. They were the ones who chased after me, and there was no chance of pregnancy since girls in estrus are kept home from school. My father and the girls' parents had to know we were fucking at least as much as we studied. They had all been horny youths once themselves.

As for the boys, I would have been glad to share my favors with them, but Pruitt claimed we were lovers. He threatened to pound to a pulp any boy who went after me. Pruitt was big and muscular and his threats were not tested. This was despite the fact he didn't actually sleep with me until the fourth quarter when he could finally pay for a wagon ride to my house from his far on the outskirts of town. With such a long build-up to our coupling I expected better. I was used to men, and Pruitt was still a youth who was fast to orgasm and could do so only once. I kicked him out of my bedroom while his wagon was still waiting.

Besides Pruitt's threat to the other boys, our class was well integrated with little bullying or segregation into cliques. In my village an awkward girl who would be ostracized in a human school was just as popular as the cleverest beauty. This was because of sex. We wanted it and freely gave it to each other, so any student who was shy or removed from the larger group would be drawn in because a girl wanted to see her breasts or a boy wanted to rub his cock against her bottom. Even ugliness had a sexual appeal to us. Everyone, regardless of gender, was seen as a potential sexual partner simply due to proximity. Was this not better than schools where children are teased and tortured?

I mention this because a girl one grade ahead above mine fluttered her eyelashes at me several times during a school day. This girl, Brettany was her name, would have been the subject of vicious bullying had she attended a human school. Her hair was unkempt, her vision poor, her clothes often stained, and she held to the out-of-date fashion of wearing striped socks over her hooves.

Still, her face was beautiful and her quiet demeanor enticed me. In the corridor after our midday recess I secreted beside her, reached up her short dress, and fondled her bottom.

"Would you like to study with me after school?" I said, giving her the code phrase that was an invitation for sex.

Brettany rarely spoke, and the same was true now. She brandished large buck teeth in a smile and nodded her head.

I nipped her ear in gratitude and got away from her before a teacher caught us. A group of girl's in the same grade as Brettany gave hoots of elation a short distance away. I saw Brettany run back into their fold, blushing with a large smile. Apparently her friends had encouraged her to chase me.

That evening I helped her out of her clothes gently in my bedroom. The girl's nervous smile remained steadfast, along with her blush. She struck me as less experienced than the others I'd had in my bed. I was tender with her, asking thrice if everything was okay and getting nods each time. She stiffened when I penetrated her. I kissed her and soothed her hair until she was calm once again, then pumped my manhood into her. The act that night had to be my sweetest and most kind. Her giggle when we were done told me she approved though I don't believe she climaxed.

Brettany rolled to the side of my bed and sat naked with her back to me. She stretched her clenched fists in the air as though giving a cheer. Then she said, "Well, I am a virgin no more!"

I gaped in shock at her and then saw the blood. You'll be pleased to know I was not so crass as to be angry with her for not telling me. I moved

beside her to kiss her lips and cuddle with her. She brought me into a tender embrace and we made love once more. This time I'm certain she reached climax.

Meanwhile, that first year, I had detentions with Renherld weekly or at the very least biweekly. Sometimes he would catch me breaking the rules and angrily announce my detention to the class. Other times he would dip his head near mine as though looking over my writing and whisper, "Stay for detention today."

"Yes, sir," I'd whisper back, surreptitiously fluttering my eyes at him.

Our later trysts lacked as much romance as the first one. Renherld kept up the ruse of disciplining me even on those days when I'd done nothing wrong. I expected a beating every time and received them with growing intensity. He became more comfortable with me and I more trusting of him.

Even when he spanked me with the paddle, I would never protest. I felt a rush of stimulation under my skin when he hurt me. It became something I strangely craved. Sometimes when he had me screaming and crying for a good ten minutes, he'd sooth my throbbing ass with caresses afterwards and I would experience a euphoric delirium. Pain faded to heat and cascading tingles. My body surged with drunkenness so potent my eyes would roll back and my flesh would tremble.

My step-father still fucked me in our home. I explained what happened at my many detentions to him and how I enjoyed it. Since I assured him I knew great pleasure, he abided my bruised ass. Still, once his hand roved over my bottom and he tsked.

"Kali, how can you like a man who's so cruel to you?"

"I don't like him," I said, and then checked myself. "Well, I mean, I don't dislike him, but I do love how me makes me feel."

"He must have walloped you rotten for you to get so black and blue."

"He whispered against my neck to ask if I could take a little more. I kissed him and told him yes. It was I who pushed him to continue."

"If he should injure you permanently…"

"He's careful, dad. That's why I trust him."

My father rolled away from me to leave the bed with a groan. "I'll be glad when you're finished with that damned school."

The blasé attitude I conveyed about Renherld was in earnest. I didn't love him. We weren't even as much as a couple as my step-father and I. Our trysts had a deadline: my graduation. I indulged in him bodily and not with my heart. It was the same as with the trysts I had with my classmates. All of it was temporary fun without meaning. Renherld gave detentions to other students besides me, even Pruitt once or twice. I believe I was his favorite or at least second favorite after Babbette. Truly such a thing didn't matter to me.

What I will say was that Renherld was granting me a master class of sexual discovery. I came into wisdom about what my body could do and what I enjoyed far earlier than my peers.

By the end of my first year I felt I'd matured a half decade. We approached summer break and were completing final exams. I was eager for a break from school. The sex was interesting, eye-opening, and pleasurable, but also overwhelming. I

needed a period of quiet recovery where I would serve no one but my step-father. You can't imagine my joy when the final bell of my first year rang.

I raced out my classroom door and then to the schoolhouse door. Before I reached it a last-year boy named Adrien hooked my arm.

"Hey there, hold it. Come with me."

He made no eye contact which would have sparked suspicion in me except every engagement like this was always about sex. I assumed Adrien wanted to set up a tryst. He was proceeding extremely clumsily if so. He should have blown me a kiss in class or pelted me with a love note. Accosting me now seemed like an afterthought.

I went with him to the water pump in the back schoolyard. Five other boys were waiting for us, all last-years. Seeing the group of larger boys, with one holding tight to my arm, made the hair on the back of my neck prick up. It was not unheard of for a gang to beat up a lone boy though it was never without motive. I couldn't fathom one for them.

Adrien released me in front of them, and a tall boy with a split lip named Clovis stepped forward.

"Look here, Kali. Tomorrow we graduate. All year long we've had a yen for you, but that selfish ass Pruitt kept you for himself. Well, we're gone from this school now. He can't do nothing to us. So why don't you come into Glider woods with us and let us have the fun we've been wanting."

My lips parted, and I looked over the motley group. Three were decent-looking fellows, with one named Maxime who was likely the equal to Pruitt in muscle. Clovis was the ugliest, but I would have still slept with him if he'd propositioned me during the school year. Adrien was short and

stocky enough to be twice my weight. Again, I would have had play with any of these boys if they'd expressed interest in me one at a time.

"You want to have me all at once?" I said.

Maxime turned up a hand. "That's the only way. This is the last time we'll have any reason to be around you. I'm off to finishing school day after tomorrow, and Padgett—" He gestured to the red-haired boy beside him. "—is going to take work at the mill in Trummell."

"We all have to get on with things," Clovis said, with a touch of a lisp. "And we have no reason to be back at school where we can see you. It's now or never."

"But all of you?" My expression had to be plaintive.

Maxime stepped beside me and wrapped an arm around my waist. "Why not? We're all friends, aren't we? No one's going to hurt you."

I swallowed at the prospect, but my cock was swelling. Why not end the year with a grand hurrah? One boy their age was completely unsatisfying. Six ought to sate me perfectly. I met Maxime's vivid green eyes.

"Do you have lubricant?"

Clovis dug a canister out of his pocket and displayed it.

I took a deep breath. "Sure," I said, managing to overcome my fear enough to smile at them. "Sounds like fun."

They cheered and gave laughs of triumph.

7 Loveless

I pause now because my beloved Richard is reading my manuscript as I write it. He turned to me with a cocked brow and said, "Are you going to describe what happened with you and those six boys?"

"Yes," I said, quite oblivious.

"Kal, you already went on about your step-father and your teacher. The press will call this deviant smut."

"Perhaps to you it is deviant smut," I said to my dear human lover, "but this is the reality of life as a faun. You said I shouldn't hold back--that it would be scandalous in any form."

He shook his head over the pages. "I know. But this may become illegal to publish. If a human woman or child should read it, you'll be accused of fostering prurient thoughts."

I slid behind him and encircled him in my arms. "What does it matter, darling? We're never going back there."

He would not look at me. "Why do you insist on describing things so graphically?"

"I suppose there's some mischievousness in my writing. You humans are so restrained. I want for my readers to learn it's not the norm everywhere. If my book will become as successful as you say, then can't I use it to influence your culture?"

He tsked. "It will be banned, but that, in its own way, shall make it even more popular."

I grinned wide. "Then what's the trouble?"

***

But perhaps my beloved Richard had a point. In diffidence to him I shall be more conservative with this description.

I followed the boys to a far point in the woods where no one would be likely to find us. There was a turned down tree, covered in soft green moss. After some kissing and caresses with all of my patrons in turn, I was stripped and bent over the log.

And so the boys took turns on me. The first was like Pruitt, and hardly stoked my excitement before finishing. The second, Maxime, went right into the previous boy's wetness and took such time fucking me the others protested for him to finish. He relinquished me without satisfaction to let them have their turns. Because of his length and heated grunts against my back, I was fully aroused as the others took me. Alas, except for one other they were all like Pruitt, filling me sometimes with just a few pumps of their hips. Maxime got back on top of me as the others were dressing to leave. He felt my nipples while humping close to my back, whispering such filth in my ear I gave throaty moans of protest. When he finished, he had the good manners to turn me over and masturbate me to climax. Then he too dressed and left me alone.

I sat on the cold ground with my bottom sloppy. My skin would be bruised from the way one boy squeezed my flanks as he thrust. I knew I might not see any of them ever again.

And I felt empty.

This was the first time that feeling plagued me. I suppose it was the cold woods and lack of tenderness in most of them. I had yielded to their needs when most of them gave no regard to my own.

I was but a trophy long denied to them which had to be won.

I'd been used. Seen as nothing but an object for their issuance.

I crawled to my feet and carried my clothes to the brook which was fueled by mountain ice. I let the cold scald me, wishing for all traces of their clammy touches to be erased.

For a long while I paced the forest, devoid of thought, for I didn't know why the act had devastated me. I cursed myself for agreeing to their request. And, still, I couldn't fathom why I hated it. A bit of fun was all it was, wasn't it?

In hindsight I knew I'd been robbed of my faunhood and made a vile receptacle of their sperm. The other trysts I'd had were always with one person, with kissing and caressing, warmth and intimacy. I could pretend there was love as the sex happened. There was no pretending this time.

This was the sort of thing that would make me despise sex. Love was what I would come to crave most of all.

8 Death

My second year was marked by the absence of the seniors and a new crop of first- years. There was no one in that class who captured Renherld's interest, so our bargain and the trysts continued. He claimed I'd grown over summer, my body longer and my legs thicker. At our first detention he took me with the abandon of reunited lovers, even dropping the ruse of punishment. His fondness for me made me grow eager for these painful sessions.

I had less to do with my classmates, however. The night in the woods afflicted me. I accepted the invitation of a boy only once that year. Why let clumsy children have me when I could be taken by skilled men? I did engage every girl who fluttered her lashes. To be the active participant in sex never lost its appeal. I preferred to be the giver rather than the taker, and with women I was always on top. I adored their lush skin and plump breasts. With them I could never feel used for I was their tender user. My position of subordinance with Renherld and my father made me need this.

By my third year I was less concerned with school than matters at home. Father fell into glooms more often. He could no longer be drawn out of bed with sex.

In early fall, I noticed rags between his bed and the wall that were crusted with phlegm.

"Are you sick, father?"

He dismissed me with a wave and turned his back to me. I defied him by fetching the doctor. In his presence father had to sit up and allow himself

to be examined. The doctor said there was nothing wrong with him.

"Have him get out of that bed and exercise some. Open his windows so he can get fresh air."

If I opened the windows, he would just close them as though he couldn't abide the air from outside to penetrate his sanctum. As for getting him to exercise, I could hardly get him to sit up and eat.

The situation was the same every day, so I forced myself to stop worrying about it. I had the more rigorous studies of my third year to consume me.

By winter I was sure he didn't eat unless I brought him food, which I only did when I returned home from school. Then he soiled his bed. I insisted he get up so I could change his bed sheets. He was unable to stand. The muscles of his legs had withered. His abdomen had loose skin where taut definition had once been.

"Father, what's happened to you!"

He waved me away and took refuge in an arm chair.

Once again I called the doctor. He said my father's greatest ailment was malaise. He had to get out of his home and exercise.

Why not ask me to move a mountain as well? I couldn't even get him to descend the stairs to eat at the table. The only thing that gave me hope was that the doctor said his skin was looking yellow, which may be due to ill-humors of the liver. He gave me extract of ginger and prescribed one tablespoon a day.

I fed it to him with his evening meal, placing all my hope on the foul-tasting medicine. Then I badgered my father to rise. He could walk no further than to his chamber pot. When I forced him

into the hallway he stumbled. His frail legs looked twisted. I got him back into his bed and hid away to cry.

I've read novels where illness appeared and was solved and treated, or the character died because they were poisoned or had consumption. There were no such answers in my life. I endured the third year of school with a father who wasted in his bed. The doctor was useless. My father's gloom never abated enough for him to find the will to fight his disease.

I remember months where I helped him to the pot, fed him spoonfuls of porridge, or carried him to his chair so I could change his bedding. His eyes became blank. He no longer heard me when I spoke to him. If I demanded he answer a question, he could only do so with a groan or a shrug.

In the summer of my third year he stopped answering at all and began to emit foam from his mouth. He would not eat. He didn't recognize me when I tried to reach him. His mind was as gone as his body, which now was easy for me to lift from the bed.

He died a shell of his former self. Tiny. Jaundiced. Curled like an infant. And it was not a shock to discover him without a pulse. I expected to find him dead every day I ascended the stairs. I'd become resigned to that morbid reality, even as it rend me inside.

I knew not what to do with a dead father on my second floor bedroom, so I went to one who I presumed dealt with death often, the doctor. This man became kind once he knew of my tragedy. Both he and the undertaker came to remove him. I sold a set of mother's figurines to pay for the funeral, as the coin from father's inheritance was

nearly gone. Dozens attended who knew me. The only ones there who'd known my father were my grandparents.

I went to them after the ceremony hoping all was forgiven.

"Who is living in that house now?" my grandmother said, looking far older than the last time I'd seen her as a young child.

"Only me."

"You should move to the orphanage," my grandfather said.

I looked at them both with shock. "Why would I?"

"So we can sell our property," grandmother said. "If you and this fool haven't destroyed it."

I grew angry. I'd just placed my father in the ground. They were wicked scavengers picking from his bones. "That house was my father's and now it's mine. Keep your greedy hands off it!"

"It's not yours," my grandmother said with a sneer. "Your father was a squatter we couldn't get rid of. You're an orphan. Go to the orphanage and give us what belongs to us."

"The hell I will!"

"What do you need such a massive house for?" my grandfather said. "In this market it could be sold for 5,000 coin."

"It's my house and you can't have it!" This was all I could scream as I ran from them.

In this, the darkest period of my life, Renherld became my savior. I wept at my desk after class the next day and intimated all the matters of my personal life which had previously been forbidden topics for us.

"That house will be entangled in your father's estate which shall be overseen by Etrian

Renherld who works in the court house. As luck would have it, he is my half-brother. Let's see him before your grandparents can get an appointment."

I snuffled and wiped my tears.

"He'll make sure you aren't kicked out, dear boy. Up, up!" He strode past me. "Let's go to him now."

I followed, feeling hopeful. It's strange who can become your ally in a time of need.

Etrian looked like a twin of Renherld who was ten years older. He was on my side as much as Renherld from the start. However, the deed of the house was in my grandmother's name. She had the legal right to take it from me.

"Here's what I can do," Etrian said, folding fingers as knobby as Renherld's. "I'll contest ownership of the house, without merit mind you, and it will tie up the matter in the system until you finish school. That should be easy enough. Then you'll have time to move on to a trade and find a new place to live."

I wept once again.

"That's better than going to the orphanage, Kali," Renherld said.

I agreed and tried to show gratitude. Beyond that facade it had all been too much. My own blood attacked me in the midst of my grief. I'd lost my anchor in life. I'd witnessed his deterioration until nearly the memory of him was corrupted.

And I never knew what it was that killed him. Not to this day, dear readers.

9 An Unpleasant Opportunity

My fourth year of school I was more withdrawn than ever. Not even the lovely girls of my class could tempt me for a tryst. Renherld and my hand were my only methods of release. The former became like a ritual for me. His beatings quieted the heartache within my soul. We'd also become as intimate as true lovers. He kissed and caressed me with as much ardor as we had during our lovemaking.

I might have believed we could be married after my graduation, except that Renherld still gave detentions to other students. I was his favored pet, but one of many. This dissolved all my romantic illusions. Each time a girl or younger boy was assigned his most extreme punishment I felt numbing stillness rather than jealousy.

Outside of school I took to the habits of my step-father, cloistering myself in the large empty house I temporarily owned. I was aware of my depression since I'd had so much exposure to it. That was the only way I measured my sanity. I knew I'd fallen into darkness, but it was temporary. A new beginning would make me right after I graduated from school.

And what would that be? I inquired about the finishing school in our town and was blindsided by the price of 500 coin per year. Who could ever afford even one year of that education?

The administrator of the school presumed I had the money because my mother's family was among the wealthiest in Schaletar. I was given a grand tour of the luxurious dormitory and massive

library. It made me ache to know I could never attend.

(The administrator did the discourtesy of following up with my grandparents. I know this because of the scathing letter grandmother sent saying she owed me nothing for I had abandoned her for the murderer of her daughter. Such cruel curses followed you would think I had only 'abandoned' her yesterday and had not been a tiny child at the time. I was pained by her words for a full week, but then considered the fact I was her only descendant. She would one day die alone with no family to comfort her.)

With higher education out of the question I looked into the trades. What interested me? At seventeen I still had no idea. I enjoyed reading, but that hardly translated into a profession. Wood work, glass work, steel work—all these trades conjured images of sweat and filth. My shapely body would grow large with muscles like Pruitt's. I found the notion so distasteful.

What of the softer trades? I would have gladly become a teacher like my dear Renherld, but this occupation required a degree I already determined I could not afford.

It was fourth quarter when I shared my indecision with Renherld after the last bell. I sat at the front of the class at the desk in his line of vision.

"So let's determine what you're suited for. Take out a sheet of paper and write your five best traits."

I tapped my pencil against my desk a few moments before finally scrawling.

1. People say I'm attractive.
2. I'm a strong reader
3. I'm a strong writer

4. I excel in most school subjects

5. I am able-bodied and in good health

Renherld scrutinized the list. "If I focus only on 2 through 4 I would say you should be a teacher."

"I'd love that, but I can't afford the schooling."

He set down the list and snuffled. "Nor could I. It took five years of work at the millery before I'd scrounged the money for my tuition."

My brow rose. "Oh."

"Let us focus on numbers 1 and 5, but let me add that you are young, which can also be marketable attribute."

"Hm."

"I believe you ought to find work that would allow you to save for tuition, and given your circumstances, it must also include room and board."

"What work could I get like this?"

"There are a few things out there, though nothing in Schaletar and most are low-paid and distasteful. But one opportunity, if it still exists, would suit you well."

"Oh?"

Renherld stood and pulled his knapsack over one shoulder. "I need to send a letter to a former student to see if what I'm thinking of is still viable. Once I'm sure I'll tell you about it."

"What? Tell me now."

He clucked his tongue and stepped in front of me. "Naughty boy." He whapped his finger where my nipple was hidden beneath my tunic. "How many times have I told you to be patient?"

I didn't get an answer until just before final exams at the end of the school year. By then I was

in a near panic about my future. Etrian had visited to tell me he could stall no longer, and papers were being processed. I had to leave soon or the magistrate would remove me by force. I explored pitifully few other avenues of employment for there was nothing I could do while still in school, and nothing that offered rooming once I graduated. All my hope lay in Renherld's possibility.

He took me to his home on the Friday before our exams were to begin. I'd been there twice before, when after school events prevented any opportunity for us to find privacy. He had a varied assortment of tools to torment me with, heightening the pain and ecstasy I always enjoyed in his care. As I entered his home, I had an involuntary reaction of arousal from the surroundings.

That night we had a simple fuck in his bed, rougher than what normal lovers might know but normal given our history. We then dressed and met in his kitchen.

"You need to get to Calico," he said, and handed me a paper.

My brows furrowed. On the paper was an address in this foreign town. "Where is Calico?"

"It's past the eastern mountains, in the land of the centeri."

I gasped. I'd seen a centerus once in my life, as an attraction in a traveling carnival. It was a muscular hornless man with legs far thicker than any faun's and a tail that was like flowing hair. His hooves were black and had no split in the middle. The hair of his legs was flat, like that of a dog, and without the brassy curls typical on faun legs. The carnival master narrated his features to the crowd all the while hinting that he was hugely endowed and with stamina unheard of in faun kind.

"Do they speak our language there?"

"Oh yes." Renherld took a sip from the tea he'd poured for both of us. "We're not terribly removed from their kind. They have an accent, and words for certain things shall be different, but you'll have no trouble communicating. My former student got on fine."

My heart quickened as he spoke. I felt his words opened doors to new and incredible possibilities.

"What will I do?"

He tapped his note. "Go to this address. It is a three story inn with two dozen rooms."

I blinked.

"I've sent letters on your behalf. Introduce yourself to the owner Mrs. Alita. She'll be expecting you. I've arranged for you to work on the grounds doing whatever they need. You'll have a place to live in the common room on the top floor. Two meals a day shall be provided. Payment is a shilling a week."

His last sentence made me deflate. "A shilling?" Father spoke of making as much in a day working as a ditch digger. "How can I ever save my tuition with such meager wages?"

He snuffled at me. "I should strike you for your lack of gratitude, but I suppose I'm feeling magnanimous tonight. You didn't let me finish."

I fixed an eager gaze on him.

"The reason you'll get this work is that you're beautiful. The inn is a rooming house for seasonal miners. They'll pay the owner to seek favors from you in the common room. Half of that money shall go to you."

The words sparked no reaction in me. I continued to stare at him, not sure that I understood, and not sure how to feel if I did.

"Kali, dear, whatever work you'd manage before pursuing your teaching career will be less than ideal. You'll endure it for the sake of your goals knowing that it's only temporary." He sipped his tea again. "I think you might excel at this work. You've the tolerance and the versatility. It will likely only be for a year."

An uneasy feeling swirled in my middle. Certainly I could do it. And certainly it would be like the episode in the woods where I let the six boys used me. Wouldn't I be broken after a year of such work?

"Why would anyone pay for favors they can so easily find for free?" I said, as if to stall.

"It's not easy in Calico. Centeri women have estrus every month with no signs to indicate it. The fear of pregnancy makes them prudish. It's expected that no woman should have sex before she's wed."

I was stunned.

"The men spend their lust on prostitutes, but those are rare enough for an unheard of demand, particularly in Calico where the city floods with unwed men who sign up for a season of labor in the mines. The men would take favors from each other, except that their god defeated a demon by dominating him in sex. A centerus man who lets another man penetrate him is called a rufine, the name of their most despised demon. They're shamed and ostracized."

"Won't I be as well?"

He shook his head. "My student said foreigners are not expected to abide their customs.

You will be adored because of your novelty, no matter what profession you partake in."

"Hm." My eyes stayed fixed on the address. I tried to think of something more to say, but had nothing. Before this conversation I had only read of prostitution in books about mystical races alien to our own. For fauns it was never a consideration since sex was freely available to most all of us. Now I had to consider it.

I thought more about my alternatives. There were none. For me to avoid sleeping in the forest and begging for my food I had to leave Schaletar. I'd only gone as far as our neighboring village Trummel in my lifetime. I had no concept of what opportunities were beyond this. They had to be fed to me by one worldlier.

Renherld presented my singular option, my only hope for an eventually prosperous future.

What choice had I but to accept it?

10 Prostitution

I'd sold mother's valuables bit by bit throughout my senior year. The first floor was devoid of furniture, which fetched little money but was sold anyway to spite my grandparents. The last thing of value was a gold serpent that fit in my hand. It had broken from the colored glass ball it once encircled. I fancied I'd keep this forever as my emergency cache. How naïve I was to think I had such a luxury.

With the serpent's money I'd buy my fare on a wagon that would take me to Trummel. From there I could buy a place on a carriage to the eastern border and then hike over the mountains twenty miles to Calico.

Since I had to go a considerable distance on foot I pared down my belongings into what could fit in a pack. All my school memorabilia went into the fireplace. I selected seven books to keep, but they wouldn't fit in my pack. So I discarded two, then two more, and then only kept two. I'd written diaries for most of my life. How I wish I still had access to them as I create this memoir. As you can guess, they went into the fire as well.

I graduated with my class and took my diploma out of its frame to curl and stow in my pack. Then I spent a final night in my home, the home of my youth. The home of my step-father. Has anyone restarted their life with a cleaner slate than I? Everything I'd ever known was stripped from my personage.

I didn't cry that night, nor when I hugged Renherld goodbye. What was our affair really? We

connected bodily, not with our minds. I couldn't tell you anything about his past besides the fact he worked at a millery to fund his finishing school.

The trip to Calico was a blur in the background of my worry and doubt. I recall getting in the carriage in Trummel and having my hooves ache as I marched to Calico.

It was an arid city far more condensed than my quaint home town; dusty, rugged, and without charm. I suppose this was due to the absence of women. I saw numerous burly centeri men gawking at me as I passed, but only one woman.

Centeri are taller than fauns and have stout legs that look as though they can kick a barn door off its hinges. They walked around the city shirtless, revealing tanned skin sometimes caked with dirt or marked with scars. Below the waist they wore pants far more concealing than the loincloths of the fauns. I felt exposed as their eyes moved over my scantily clad groin. Their pants had holes in the back where their flowing tails could come out. The cobbles of the walk made their large round hooves thud with every step. That sound, and the shouts of hawkers at wheeled kiosks selling wares, filled the main street.

I asked one such hawker for directions to the inn and he pointed to the end of the block which was the intersection of the town's two main roads. The inn had a vast wrap-around porch with centeri men filling seats at small round tables. They ceased their games and chatter to eye me as I ascended the stoop. One man clapped and yanked his companion close to whisper about me. I didn't like his askew smile.

Inside was a restaurant with more round tables and chairs. Only half a dozen men filled

these seats as they required the purchase of food or drink. The leftward wall was lined with a bar where three men holding tall tankards of ale turned in their stools to look at me. Straight ahead was the counter of the inn's management. Two centeri women, one middle-aged with deep jowls, the other plump and likely only six years older than me, manned the post. I approached sheepishly.

The older woman caught sight of me before the younger. She nudged the other's shoulder to get her to look. Now both sets of light brown eyes were upon me. The heavy younger woman, a blonde who I would find had a tail that matched her hair, parted her lips wide.

I cleared my throat before them. "Could I speak to Mrs. Alita?"

"That's me," the older woman said.

"My friend Mr. Renherld...he...I'm supposed to have..."

"I know who you are."

The woman beside her giggled. "Would you look at this one!"

The former remained transfixed, looking me up and down. "Yes, I think you pass. Once you've scrubbed the filth off of you, that is." She tipped her nose at the other. "Get Erwan."

The woman lifted a bar next to them to exit the counter. She clopped her hooves down a corridor near us, which led out of the restaurant to a set of dark wood stairs.

The older woman recaptured my attention. "What's your name?"

"Kali Hartswit."

She scrawled it down. "What do you think you'll be doing here, Kali?"

I fumbled for my words. "A variety of things."

She fixed a sharp gaze on me. I noted that her hair color was the same as the younger woman's, but graying at the temples. "What did Mr. Renherld tell you?"

I brought one arm across my front to scratch the opposite elbow. "He said I'd work where needed around the hotel…and service patrons. Patrons who…"

"Who want to fuck." Her eyes narrowed. "That's clear isn't it?"

I swallowed and nodded.

"You're not helping around the hotel. I have all the staff I need. You're here for the men. That's all you'll do."

I took a second, but I forced another nod.

"Look, you've come all the way from faun-land and I don't want a problem. Are you up for this work or not?"

"It's fine."

She snuffled at me. "Well, we'll see. Consider yourself on probation. I've got no use for a blushing virgin."

"I'm definitely not that."

"Good looks are not all you need to succeed here. I want my customers to be happy."

"Understood."

Her stern eyes scrutinized me a moment more, then she laid three colored wooden cards on the counter. "It's a shilling a week, lunch and dinner, and a bedroom upstairs. Men will buy one of these cards for a visit with you." She touched each one in turn. "Red is for sex. Blue is for oral sex. Yellow is a half-hour of your time."

"A half-hour…?"

"They don't always want to fuck. Sometimes they want someone to talk to. These men are far from their homelands, they crave surrogate wives and mothers to comfort them."

I blinked at the cards as the words permeated me.

"We split everything 50/50. Red is two gold coins. Blue is one gold coin, so two-and-a-half shillings for you. Yellow is two shillings, so we each get one. I'll keep track of your share and deposit it into the bank with your pay each week."

My brow twitched. "Oh."

"You'll open a bank account tomorrow at the Calico Trust." She pursed her lips. "Now, if you make it through probation, your contract is for one year. While you're under contract, you can withdraw only 10 percent of your account balance out each week. You don't get the full balance until you've completed your contract."

My stomach twisted. Should I find the work unbearable my money would be held hostage.

"I'm not going to put the time into training you just to have you bolt two months in. I need a year. A solid year."

I nodded once more. "Understood."

A black-haired centerus with a small rat-like face and dressed in ill-fitting finery approached from down the hall. He stood outside the counter beside Alita.

"This is the new comfort worker, Erwan," she said while gesturing to me. "Get him situated. Teach him what we need."

Erwan spoke without looking at her. "I'm expecting clients."

"Let him see what you do. He's as green as they come. Oh, and if he runs off in a day, I'll hold you accountable."

Erwan scoffed. He turned to walk down the corridor again. Alita shooed me with both hands in his direction. I donned my heavy pack and caught up to him at the stairs.

"You ought to start tomorrow because I have more customers than I can deal with and they're getting sick of waiting two or three days to get with me."

"Huh."

"I can take the mean ones while you're getting settled in."

"Mean ones?"

"I mean stupid ones. Annoying ones." His flowing black tail swished in my face.

"Huh."

We ascended the stairs to a corridor lined with three doors on each side. Erwan continued around the banister to another set of stairs.

"They all want to fuck your ass. No one ever buys a yellow card. The blue cards are always angry they couldn't afford to just fuck you. They don't even want to look at you while you're sucking them."

I felt a surge of dizziness. "Ugh."

"Maybe it will be different for you. I don't know. I will always be a fucking rufine as far as they're concerned. Maybe they'll all want you going forward so they don't have to be around me."

"Hmm."

Again we rounded the banister at the top of the stairs to ascend to another floor. I was getting winded.

"After your first week go to the bank and get out your ten percent. You're going to need lanolin tincture for your skin."

"What? Why?"

"Because you have to bathe after every fuck and it dries you out. You'll want a robe to wear when you're working too. No sense dressing and undressing each time. Especially at night when they all come in and you have one after the other."

I rubbed my forehead.

The top floor had a small landing with a door. We entered a large open room with two rows of beds. Four men were scattered on them, some sleeping, some sitting and reading, and one digging muck from his hooves with a stick. These occupied beds had bags and loose clutter surrounding them. The back of the room was cordoned off by floor-to-ceiling curtains. Erwan opened the split down the center and led me in.

Here was a proper bedroom, with a large bed, nightstand, chest of drawers, and a vanity with a tall mirror. A fourth of the room was tiled with a bathtub in it. There were hot and cold taps. I was unsure how they managed to get water to this top floor.

"Here's your room," Erwan said.

I blinked. All this for me? I went to the bed to dump my backpack on it.

"Don't let the curtain fool you into thinking you have any privacy. These bastards will peak in right when you're in the thick of it. That's why I insisted on a proper room."

My shoulders sank. "Oh."

Erwan snuffled and turned away. "I've got to see my client. It's just sucking his dick. No talk.

Nothing fancy. You don't really need a lesson on that, do you?"

I shook my head.

"Good. Mrs. Alita told me to be comforting, to be their sweetheart. That's all rubbish. They don't want to talk to me."

"Do you think it's because you're a rufine? Maybe they'll want to talk to me."

He scoffed. "Maybe. Anyway, I have to go." He parted the curtain but then paused. "Oh, get washed up then go to the kitchen on the first floor in the restaurant. Lunch is at noon and dinner at 5. I'm sure you can start tomorrow, right?"

I shrugged.

"Of course you can." He left me.

The tub filled with heavenly hot water. I wanted to languish, but the meager curtain made me fear onlookers. I covered myself with the large towel hanging on a hook and dressed underneath it.

Next I emptied my belongings into the dresser. A wind-up clock on top of it told me I had a half hour before dinner.

A man peeked into my curtains. I froze and met his gaze.

"Hello," he said through a smile. "You're a new comfort worker?"

I nodded.

"Well, are you available to comfort me?"

"I think I start tomorrow."

He clucked his tongue. He had long black hair, a regal face, and thick muscles. "Pity. Can I make an appointment then?"

"I'm not sure how things work here yet."

He let himself into my room. "Normally one just buys a card at the desk and comes up to see

you. But with just one fellow working here he's always busy, so we've had to make appointments."

"Oh." I focused on my dresser. "Is it safe to leave my things up here?"

"Sure. The men who rent this room have to pile their stuff around their beds. No one takes anything, well not usually. We're all the same, you see. Just here to do our work in the mines, make our money, and get home. It's a lonely lot. But you're very pretty. The best I've seen in all my years working here."

A smile germinated on my face without my control. "Thank you." I'd reverted to my flirty faun ways.

"Why don't you let me be your first client? I'll buy a yellow card. What do you say?"

"That's just the thing. I have no idea what to do. You're going to pay two shillings for a half-hour of my time. How can I make that worth it for you?"

"Why don't I show you? I'll teach you what we want. It will be fun. Plus I'll get to look at your beautiful face without creeping around this curtain."

I laughed.

"So what do you say?"

"Okay." I bowed my head coyly. "But I need to have dinner. Can you book me an hour from now?"

He gleamed straight white teeth in a smile. "Wonderful. I'm Soan, by the way."

"Kali."

Downstairs I was directed to the back of the kitchen. The younger woman I'd seen before and two men shared a table. I got a bowl of vegetable stew and bread roll and joined them. The plump blonde was speaking.

"Mother got a new man."

Two men across from her looked up.

"What? Where?" said one.

The woman jabbed her thumb at me. "Right there."

They both laughed.

"That's not a man," said the other who had rust colored hair and crooked teeth. "That's a little lady showing off her caboose."

The three laughed. I remained stone-faced.

"No, but really, you need to get yourself some pants," the woman said. "You can't be walking around like that."

I looked down at my loincloth and grumbled. "I don't have money for a tailor."

"You'll make plenty of money your first week." This man had white hair, but was the same age as the woman. It was parted down the middle showing pink scalp.

"I'll only be able to withdraw ten percent."

Both men tilted their heads up with enlightenment.

"Oh right. So Mrs. Alita thinks this one will run away, huh Camille?" the rust haired one said.

"Wouldn't you?" She turned to me. "I'm Camille." She pointed to the white haired man "This is Ethan." Her finger moved to the rust-haired. "This is Gabin."

"Kali," I said.

"Kali the faun," Gabin said. "First time out of your village?"

"The first time out this far."

"Do you know what these men are going to do to you, sweet Kali?" Ethan said. Camille burst with laughter.

"They're going to fuck me."

Now all three laughed.

Gabin squeezed my shoulder. "Oh, I like you. You look a sweet and innocent, but we all know how you fauns really are."

I looked the three over. "And what do you do here?"

Ethan pointed to himself. "Kitchen staff." He jabbed his thumb at Gabin and then Camille. "Housekeepers."

"There's Philipe too, who does maintenance and runs the boiler," Camille said. "He's around here somewhere."

Alita thrust herself through a swinging door to the side of us. She clopped to me and I felt like cringing. The matron exuded harrowing authority.

"Did Erwan show you what to do?"

I pursed my lips. "Not really."

She looked upwards and fumed. "Well there's a man who says you agreed to take his appointment tonight."

"Soan?"

"Yes. So you'll take him?"

I nodded.

"Wow, Soan jumped right on him, didn't he?" Camille said.

"Do you know what to do with the card when he gives it to you?" Alita said.

"No."

She fumed again. "That damned Erwan! There's an open pipe in the floor of your room beside your bed. Put the cards down the pipe so they come back to me. Otherwise a man might take it when you're not looking and use it twice."

My brow furrowed. "Okay."

"And don't give sex to yellow cards. They want sex they have to buy blue or red. Got it?"

"Yes."

"Because if you do it once they'll keep taking advantage of you. And set the alarm on your clock so you don't go over a half-hour."

"Yes, madam."

"Erwan should have told you all this!" She shook her head at Camille before looking back at me. "When the other men see you're taking appointments they're going to want to buy cards. So are you working tonight or what?"

I carved the skin off one cuticle. "Sure."

"He needs pants, mom," Camille said.

"I'll see about that tomorrow. You must bathe after every red card and rinse your mouth after every blue. There's a pitcher of mint water in your room."

"Understood."

Mrs. Alita hovered as though thinking of more to say. "Well. All right. I'll see how you are tomorrow." She left.

Ethan rose with his dirty bowl in hand. "Someone's going to be busy tonight."

Camille giggled again. "Stop it, you."

11 Initiation

I found the pipe beside the wall and dropped the yellow card Soan gave me. There was a black card on the floor near it. I picked it up.

"I wonder what this is for."

"You kick that one in the hole if you need help."

I cringed and set it back down.

Soan was reclining on the bed with his arms braced behind his head. "Don't worry. You can cry out and the men in the common room will come to your rescue. Any fool who hurts you will have his face bashed in."

I reclined on my side facing him feeling strange giddiness. All Erwan's foreboding was erased by this friendly good-looking client. I felt in my element.

"So," I said with a demure smile, "what should I do to make you happy?"

His grin crinkled his eyes. "There was a faun woman who worked here three years ago. She had to be past forty and was round and soft. When she had a client, she would turn into the sweetest girlfriend. She'd wear a silk lace chemise and panties and smile at you as though you were her long lost love. Maeva was her name. Maeva would light up her face with a huge smile and say, 'There's my dear one! Come to the bed sweetheart. You must be so tired. Let me rub those thick shoulders of yours.'" His voice went up an octave as he quoted her. "She'd rub you all over and give hot wet kisses. She'd ease you into sex as though she wanted it. Then she moaned and trembled.

She'd make her clients climax so fast with her passion. Even when she was sucking you, she made sounds through her nostrils as though it was her favorite thing to do. I had a yellow card with her and she took down the straps of her chemise and let me lick and fondle her breasts. She cuddled against me, coaxing me to tell her all my troubles. When I left, I'd make another appointment right away. Maeva made life out here bearable. She was everyone's darling. She put a light in all our eyes. And if anyone crossed her…" He shook his head. "They'd learn their lesson fast."

"That sounds nice." I reached out and stroked his gleaming black hair. "I'd like to be like Maeva," I said, only half-lying. "You men need someone like her, and you were kind to her in return. Erwan made it seem as though I couldn't be happy here."

Soan's eyes rolled. "Oh Erwan. Don't listen to his self-pitying rufine stories. We've had rufine's here before. If they embraced the job and were sweet to us, we would be good to them. Erwan let's everyone know he hates what he does. He sneers and barks at us to hurry. He has no charm. With him you have to close your eyes and pretend you're with someone else."

"Hm." My brows pinched. "Why did he take this job?"

"Laziness. Work in the mines is backbreaking and only pays a shilling a day to the season workers. Erwan can make four coin a night as a comfort worker. He hoards his money and then runs away to spend it all the second his contract is up. A few months later he'll crawl back to beg Sara for another chance."

"I see." I moved my hand from his hair to his bare arm and soothed him up and down. "Thank you for teaching me. I'll be a much better comfort worker than Erwan. I promise."

This made his eyes glimmer. "Well let's see. How about a kiss?"

I rolled onto him and joined our mouths. Soan's strong arms enclosed around me, making me feel warm. My body automatically prepared for sex. I couldn't help for my erection to hit his thigh.

He broke our merged tongues to laugh at me. "Oh, yes. You're adorable. What say you let me see it? And your pretty chest too."

I crawled off the bed to strip for him. The only thing that made me hesitate was the scant curtain separating me from the boarders in the room. I convinced myself I should not be bashful. I would embrace this job. To be another Erwan would make me sick.

Soan had me turn around and then moved close to grope my bottom. His large warm hand squeezed one side, then the other.

"Gods what a pretty ass. Does this bother you? Being touched?"

I smiled over my shoulder at him. "Not when it's you."

He shuddered with contentment. "What a fast learner you are. Come here."

I crawled into his arms, accepting more kisses while pressed against him. He pulled the blanket over us.

"In case we have any spectators."

"Thank you." Oh, how I hoped all my clients would be as courteous.

He pushed his hand between my thighs and felt my balls. My cock was now stiff enough to point at my navel. I began to tremble.

"Have you had a man inside you before?"

I nodded, scarcely able to focus.

"Let me buy a red card tonight. I'm aching for you."

I brought my lips to his ear. "Run down and buy it now. I'll add the rest of your time on for the yellow card. You should get it before someone else books me."

Soan gave me a searing kiss. The sudden passion startled me. Then he leapt up from the bed and galloped away through the curtains.

I sighed. The echo of his hand was still on my tense balls. How nice it would be to have Soan as my first customer.

He returned with a contented grin. "You're booked for the rest of the night."

My lips parted.

Soan flashed a red card. "So I paid the difference to upgrade my card."

I clapped my hands below my chin. Soan unbelted his pants and yanked them down. The elation in my face evaporated. His cock was enormous, with the length and girth of my forearm.

He climbed onto the bed with the thick organ bobbing between his legs. "Let me give you another lesson. You need to see to lubrication. Your patrons might not, or may not use enough."

I forced myself to nod and took the lubricant from the nightstand. My words came out nervously as I greased my bottom.

"I've never had someone as large as you."

Soan tipped his head up and then nodded. "Ah yes. I think Maeva mentioned something about that."

"You're twice as large as anyone I've ever been with."

He soothed my leg. "I'm average as far as centeri go. How lucky for you I'll be your first. We have most of an hour before your next appointment. I'll break you in gently."

I sat up and kissed him, feeling as lucky as he said. My erection had flagged from fear. Soan tickled his fingers up my flanks while melding his hot tongue to mine. It took only moments of his lover-like care for me to relax once more. His hand went between my legs, feeling both my testicles. Then he gripped my shaft and pumped me. I gave a nasal moan while we still kissed.

"Rub the lubricant on my cock now." He spoke with our eyes and moist lips close. "You shouldn't expect the men to do it themselves. They'll be too eager when they see you."

"Right."

I slathered the harrowing organ using both hands. This was my chance to show I truly was experienced. I massaged his cap and balls in a way that made Madio moan in the past. Soan grunted with flared teeth.

"That's it, little minx."

He grabbed under my thighs before I was done, making my back flop onto the bed. Then he snatched the two pillows behind me and put them under my hips. My legs bent back naturally from the angle, granting full view of my gleaming anus. Soan grunted again with approval. He pressed his cock against my hole entering me with an upward slant. I'd never made love in this position before.

I hid my contorted face with my hand as he pushed harder and harder against my ring until finally his oiled cap popped in.

"Is that all right, Kali?" he said, sounding breathless.

"Mm hm." It actually hadn't hurt as much as I expected. My stretched ring throbbed and felt full to the brink. I hadn't been injured, however, and Soan kept still to allow my body to adapt.

His hands closed over my groin from both sides, rubbing around my cock while two thumbs dug in the sublime place beneath my balls.

"There's a good boy. Breathe deep for me."

I obeyed but with a quiver. His hand now distracted me from the discomfort of my ass.

"Centeri are oblivious of their girth. I want you nice and stretched for your next customer. They won't mean to hurt you, but they might."

I peeked up at him with a sensual flicker of my lashes. "You're so kind, Soan."

His hand rubbed over my balls and mashed the underside of my shaft. "No, no. Just showing common decency."

I took another quavering breath. "Fuck me, Soan."

His grunt came with an ecstatic clench of his eyes, then he pushed into me a quarter inch a second. The reason for the position became clear with a jolt and a gasp. His cock crushed right against the sweet spot inside of me, shooting overwhelming pleasure through my entire body. My nipples hardened. My hooves swirled. The moan I let out had to be heard throughout the entire common room.

"There we are," he said with his chest heaving. "You precious thing."

Another half inch went inside, heightening what was already overpowering rapture. I flailed with one leg, twisting my hip to escape the heat at the back of my groin. When I tipped sideways drops of clear issuance spilled from my slit.

Without thinking I reached for my cock. Soan caught my hand. I opened my eyes to cast a stricken look toward him.

"Sweetness, you've got four other men to serve tonight."

"Four?"

"As much as I want to see you pleasuring yourself, it would be a disservice to you. Every man will expect to see you excited and will be disappointed if you're not. Save your climax for your last appointment or see to it afterwards alone."

My expression grew solemn. "Oh."

He leaned over to give my swollen nipple a kiss. A ticklish sting cascaded through my chest.

"I'm not trying to make you sad, beautiful. Just being pragmatic. Men are paying for you to pleasure them—not the other way round."

"Ohh." My voice was louder now. He'd gotten through to me. "I'm sorry."

"Why be sorry? I'm depriving myself by telling you. Damn, what I wouldn't give to see you squirming in orgasm."

I hugged my arms around him and leaned up for a kiss. "Be my last appointment next time."

He licked my tongue. "Sounds nice."

His warmth separated from my tremulous body as he sat up once more. His cock continued to burrow inside. I could only moan and thrash my head to the side while subdued by the onslaught of pleasure

Soan pressed until he'd filled me beyond reason. I could scarcely notice the throbbing of my ring with the pressure he put on my sweet spot. As he withdrew, and his slick organ mashed over it, I whimpered my moans. Bad manners or not, I might climax without even touching myself. By the time he could fuck me with measured strokes I felt prickly heat at the base of my cock, begging for release. I rubbed my nipples for want of something to touch.

"Oh, that's nice, but look in my eyes more, sweetness. Let me know your reaction is all for me."

I opened my eyes to obey. It would be the only time I needed such obvious instruction. Moaning and squirming while looking into his eyes made the act more erotic. I was giving myself to him like a true adoring lover.

The alarm went off on my clock to indicate his time was over. Soan's torso muscles flexed, and he fucked me at a faster rhythm for ten more strokes before gushing hot sperm inside of me. My body was shivering for release now. It felt so good, and I was so unused to depriving myself.

My briefly built enthusiasm for the job dissolved. What fun was sex if I couldn't climax?

He closed over me for a final bout of kissing.

"Clean yourself quickly," he said with his breath hitting my lips. "It's best not to keep the next man waiting. Especially after your moans have him worked up into a frenzy.

I hugged him once more. "You were such a good teacher."

I got into the tub while Soan dressed. Luxuriating in the warm water wasn't possible. I sponged my ass clean, expelling all I could, and

then pulled the plug to drain it. Once dry I donned only my loincloth and returned to the bed. As if on cue a head poked into my curtains.

It was my rust-haired co-worker Gabin brandishing a blue card. He grinned at my shock.

"Figured I'd get you before you get sad and run away."

I made myself laugh at him. "I'm not going to run away, silly. Now get over here."

12 The Comfort Worker

I took Soan's schooling to heart and tried to turn myself into Maeva as much as was possible while keeping some dignity. That night all my clients were kind and happy to see I would give them the solace they so needed. I received none of the coldness Erwan described. I believed Soan's estimation of him to be true.

When my clock read 4 in the morning Camille entered my curtain. "Can you do one more red?"

I shrugged and nodded. Why wouldn't I?

She left and was replaced by another male miner who reciprocated my loving attitude. This made five for the night, all reasonably pleasant. My erection abated during my final bath without any satisfaction. I was too exhausted to masturbate.

Being charming and feigning love was tedious. My body's response to the sex became a nuisance. It wasn't mutual lovemaking, just letting myself get fucked. There was never any climax for me.

I fell asleep filled with a miasma of emotion. The only good thing was that I was no longer clenched with dread. I knew what was expected of me.

"Knock, knock," Alita said before entering my curtained space the next day.

I sat up drowsily to meet her.

She went over to inspect my tub which seemed to be an excuse to talk without looking at me. "Everyone likes you. Keep it up."

"Thanks."

"It's noon. You should get up now so you don't miss lunch. Normally we end appointments at 4am so you can get enough sleep. I know you went past that last night."

I pulled on my tunic. "It's fine."

She snuffled at me. "Well eat your lunch fast because we need to go to the bank and the tailor to get you some pants. I'm giving you an advance on your pay to cover it."

"Oh, good." I hopped up and followed her out.

The bank and tailor was in walking distance to the inn. I got a book marked with the first deposit of 4 gold coins. The fifth I'd earned was presented to the tailor. Alita instructed me to wait as he crafted the garment so I wasn't walking around in the loincloth anymore. I had to go back to the inn afterwards as I had clients waiting.

Sitting in the tailor's gave me a chance to decompress. I'd made 5 coin in one night. If this was the norm I'd have…what? Eighteen hundred coin in a year? Tuition was only 500 a year and two years to graduate. I'd have money to spare.

One year. That's all you have to do.

Even if it filled me with a forlorn emptiness, surely I could endure anything for a single year. I would do the work and look forward to putting this experience in my past.

My days started at noon, when I woke and went downstairs for lunch. My first client would come at one. If he was a red or blue card, which I preferred, it would take only fifteen minutes. Foreplay was a brief greeting that made them think I wanted to see them, then touching and enticement for them to get on with it. I'd bathe in a shallow tub for red cards, or gargle with mint water for blue,

and sometime change my sheets if they'd been soiled. Then I was onto the next and the next.

I became used to sex without a climax. What I did there was work, nothing more, and my libido sank. I was a hot-blooded faun, at yet I no longer masturbated. Weeks of endless sex, where I became a vessel for sperm, made all sex distasteful for me. I dreamed of love and a lover where sex could be meaningful and truly mutual. This was a dream I put aside while I toiled.

By working all my waking hours I could easily make 7 or 8 coin a day. I wanted it to be like this. When a new client appeared I became the sultry whore Kali. The real Kali, who just wanted to go to school and find someone to love in earnest was stuffed in a compartment where his woeful thoughts would not hinder my performance.

A month passed. I looked my sallow reflection in the mirror and burst into tears. Why did I cry? I couldn't put it into thoughts. The sadness within me simply bubbled up and broke free. I collected myself and went downstairs to Alita's counter.

"I'd like a day off."

She eyed me and then pulled out my appointment book. I expected protest, but, then, I was earning her so much money. I'm sure she obliged me to prevent me from leaving.

"How about day after tomorrow? There's no appointments for you yet."

I sighed. "Good. Yes. Please."

My response struck her. "I could give you a day off each week if you wanted. You don't have to work every single day. I was going to mention that."

Sure you were. "Yes. I'd like that."

"So every Tuesday, starting with day after tomorrow."

"Wonderful. Erwan can pick up the slack on those days."

She scoffed. "Didn't you hear? He left two weeks ago."

My brow rose.

"I'm sure he'll come crawling back when he needs more money."

"Er, speaking of that. I haven't had a chance to go to the bank since you took me when I first got here. I'd like some spending money for my day off."

She put away my appointment book and pulled out another register. "I told you you could withdraw ten percent a week until your contract is done, then you get the balance. If you haven't been making withdraws you've missed your chance for these past weeks." She scrawled on the register while whispering numbers to herself. "I've made seven deposits for you. There's still what's owed for this week, but I'll deposit that on Monday. You have $239 coin in the bank."

My eyes bulged. "Really?"

She gasped at me. "You haven't been keeping track? Well, lucky for you I'm an honest woman who would never cheat my workers."

I believed her. She could have told me 150 coin and I would have thought it correct. I truly had no idea.

"Thank you, Mrs. Alita."

"It would be acceptable for you to take out 24 coin. I wouldn't keep that in your room, however. It could be stolen."

"No, I wouldn't need that much. Just two coin for pocket money."

"That's a lot of pocket money."

I laughed in a somewhat crazed manner as that was the state of my constitution. "I know! Who would think I'd make so much!"

She gave me a glimmer of a smile. The first I'd seen from her. "Well, you've earned it. If you're going to the bank go quick. You've a client at 1."

"I'll go on my day off."

Tuesday came and I luxuriated in my bed long past noon. I didn't care about missing lunch. I had plenty enough money for a fine meal at the other restaurant in town some clients had told me about. After visiting the bank I ambled to the apothecary for the lanolin tincture Erwan mentioned. I wouldn't get a robe, since my loincloth served just as well. A few clients tipped their noses in greeting as I passed them on the street. At last I went to the restaurant at the far end of the main street to indulge in my expensive meal.

The greeter blocked me with his hand before I could enter. He gripped my shoulder a bit too hard and leaned down to whisper.

"We can't allow a comfort worker to dine here. This is a family establishment."

My breath left me.

"One wouldn't wish for a client to see you while dining with his wife."

Oh. The explanation helped me to recover. I presumed all my clients were single mine workers, but how was I to know?

"If you wish to order from the menu we'll prepare a bagged meal for you to take away, but I ask you wait next door at the winery."

"Okay," I said quietly. "Sorry. I didn't know."

"Not at all." He patted my shoulder.

"If you would please prepare a fine meal, with your recommendations, I'll wait in the winery for it to be delivered." I placed a shiny gold coin in his hand. This was five days wages for a miner, and had to be three times as much as their finest dinner. I felt the need to show off after his admonishment.

"Absolutely!" he said, no longer whispering. "I'll have the king's meal prepared, with every embellishment." He unlocked a money drawer and gave me two shillings and five pennies in change.

With that I went to the winery, which I presumed didn't have any wives or children who needed to be protected from me. It was a shop built into an alley, so was scarcely six feet wide. The purveyor bowed as I entered. I went past his counter to be surrounded by two high wooden shelves filled with tall bottles or jugs of every color. A few men browse while smoking acrid cigars. They gave me the customary stares before returning their focus to the bottles.

I looked over the selection within reach completely at a loss.

The owner, a centerus with the height of a child yet the girth of a man (a type of dwarfism which also occurred among fauns) came over with a yellow toothed smile.

"So you must be the new worker at our lovely inn."

I blushed. The incident at the restaurant had made me coy. "Yes."

"Well you're a celebrity here. How magnificent to meet you. You must let me help you choose a few bottles."

His fawning (for lack of a better word) led me to make some deductions in my head. He knew

I was a comfort slave. He knew I had money. Hence, he was buttering me up to get me to part with some money.

But what was wrong with that? I would rather be treated like a wealthy noble than a whore who was unworthy of dining in public. I reciprocated his smile.

"I know little about spirits. I've drunken ale, that's about all."

"Well let me give you an education. One your age should graduate from ale to wine." He bent down and opened a compartment near the floor that had looked like wainscoting. Several half-empty bottles were pulled out. He set one on a tray and unhooked a metal cup attached to his collar to place it beside the bottle.

"Now this is our sweetest wine. If you're new to wine it will taste like candy to you." He poured a small amount into the hourglass shaped cup and handed it to me. I would have mentioned I didn't care for sweets (few fauns do) but I was too keen to try it.

There was sweetness that hit my tongue first, but then a sharp tinny taste that made me grimace.

"Not fond of the bite, I see. Let me give you something smoother."

This next wine was dark as mulberry juice and went down as slippery as butter. There was no harsh taste at the end, only warmth in my stomach.

"I like that. What does a bottle cost?"

"Why for that blend only half a shilling." (This was half a day's wages in the mines).

"I'll buy that one, then."

"Splendid! But why stop there? You've not even tried a white yet."

For the half hour it took for me to receive my meal I tried a good dozen wines and purchased five bottles. I also bought a corkscrew and two crystal glasses. After living in relative poverty during my final school year it felt magnificent to spend money so freely. The bottles were delivered to my room at the inn since it was too much for me to carry. They arrived shortly after I came back with my meal. I made myself a picnic on my bed, pouring freely from the bottle of buttery dark wine.

I'm sure you think you know where this is leading, dear reader. No, I never became a drunk, per say. I drank more than one at my tender age should, but never so much that I was impaired at my work. On Tuesdays I would indulge to drunkenness, grateful to fall into that abyss. Ethan, my coworker, taught me to drink equal parts water with my wine to avoid any pain the next morning. After drinking to double vision on Tuesday, I would be revived enough in spirit the next day to resume my work with fresh gusto. Who can fault me for seeking whatever escape I found available?

I also did not squander the money I worked so dearly to obtain. I took two shillings as a weekly allowance. The rest was allowed to collect in my bank account.

13 The Pervert

Six months in, Alita spoke to me about renewing my contract for another year. It was all I could do not to retch in front of her. Here I was celebrating being half-way done with my torture, and she suggested I double it.

"I'd like to start school as soon as my year is up."

"If you were to stay another year you could afford school, a house, a carriage, and more. What does a teacher make, anyway? Two shillings a week?"

"I'll think about it."

I learned that the hotel made 80 coin a month from the rooms and the restaurant. They were making over 200 more by splitting my comfort worker wages. I felt guilt over my unwillingness to stay. Some, but not enough to sign a new contract.

To my dismay all my regulars disappeared and a crop of new men took their place. I learned that men only worked in the mines half a year at a time due to a law passed long ago in the village. The dust of the mines was damaging to their health and was even rumored to be able to kill a faun in only three months. By working only half a year the men recovered their health and stamina during their off season. I must add that I had no reason to think the mines were making them sick. They all seemed the picture of health when the visited me.

It was annoying to start over with strangers, but only for a few weeks. I found my rhythm once again with men who quickly became comfortable with me.

It was my eighth month in when Alita approached me during my lunch once more.

"So," she said, hovering beside me as I ate, "two brothers run the mine, each taking half a year's work at a time."

"Oh good gods," Camille said. "Is Hugo back?"

"He's been back," her mother said, "but only just found out we had a new faun comfort worker."

Ethan and Camille giggled at each other. Gabin kept eating. I was unsure what kept him from teasing me along with them. (It might have to do with Ethan and Camille becoming a couple.)

"Anyway, he would like an appointment with you at his home."

I looked at her with a stitch in my brow. "Oh."

"It would be for a full day."

My confusion amplified. "What?"

"And he would pay fifty coin. Twenty-five for each of us."

I blinked at her.

"Though since you're not using my facilities, I would be willing to let you have 30 coin this time. I mean, I should still get a hefty cut because he only knew of you because you work here. You're in my employ."

I turned up my hands and shook my head. Had I complained about the distribution? Twenty-five coin was what I made in four days.

"What does he want with me?"

Alita's ample chest rose and fell with a sigh. Camille was kind enough to jump in.

"He's a pervert." Camille still grinned. "He wants to inflict all manner of wickedness on your body."

"Not all manner." Alita glowered at her. "He won't have sex with you, oral or otherwise. He just likes…" She looked around the kitchen at a loss. "Games."

"I'm fine with games," I said, raising everyone's brows, "but am I going to be injured? Bruised? Suffocated? Will he stop what he's doing if I ask? There are certain limits to what I'll abide, especially when I've not even the benefit of the black card to push down the pipe." (By the way, dear reader, I never had to use that card during all my time in Alita's employ.)

Alita pulled a chair to the end of the table and sat. She folded her hands in front of her and took a deep breath. "All right. I will tell you this. We had a woman faun here a short while back and she took the appointment with Hugo once and only once. She was disturbed by it. I think it's why she didn't renew her contract."

I groaned.

"I'm just trying to be honest with you. Now Erwan, you remember Erwan?"

I nodded.

"He said yes every time Hugo asked for him. I think they had a dozen appointments or so."

"A pity he's not here to tell me what happened."

"Erwan was a pig." Gabin spoke without looking up from his food. "He didn't care what Hugo did to him. He just cared about the money."

I sneered. "I won't abide foul things being done to me, with urine or—"

Camille's face contorted. "Eww!"

"It's nothing like that," Alita said. "He's very clean."

I swallowed. "I'm not comfortable taking such a risky appointment."

"Good for you," Gabin said, with genuine admiration.

"Kali." Something in Alita's voice made me look at her. "He could close this inn if he wanted. Hugo and his brother Jules run this town. Jules is the governor and Hugo is the chief magistrate."

"You don't think he'd do something to us do you?" Camille said.

"Hugo likes having access to comfort workers. That's the only reason we're exempt from the law." Alita looked at me. "We're the only business allowed a comfort worker permit in Calico."

My face clenched. "Then tell him I'm afraid. Appeal to him as one centerus to another. Tell him I'm fragile and terrified to meet his request. Put the blame on me and not you."

"I'll do that, Kali, but it won't stop him. Protest will make him want you more."

"But since you can't force me, make it clear it's out of your hands."

"Indeed. Out of mine and into his. He'll come here and try to convince you in person."

I shrugged. "Good. Then he could tell me what he means to do and reassure me. If it's not beyond my limits I'll oblige him, provided he's trustworthy."

"Is he trustworthy?" Gabin said.

"Now don't start that." Alita jabbed her finger in Gabin's face. "He's obviously not too terrible or Erwan wouldn't have kept going back to

him." She stood. "I'll send word with his man and see what happens."

What happened was I had someone walk through my curtain while I was servicing a blue card. I gaped back at the man who had oiled black hair, a mustache, and far apart eyes that bulged from his wide face. I stopped sucking and drew breath to scream. My customer grabbed a clump of my hair purposefully to make me look at him.

"That's my boss."

Oh. So it was Hugo the pervert. Still, I stood up from my knees and faced him.

"Sir, I must ask you wait outside the curtain."

He made an unsavory grin. "Oh, don't mind me."

"It's all right," my client said, without conviction.

I spoke louder. "I'm afraid it's not. Wait outside."

For a few moments we stood at an impasse. Hugo remained grinning at me in front of my curtain. I stood glaring at him. Finally he bowed and stepped outside.

"How rude," I said, while kneeling once again.

"You sure knew how to handle him." The miner laughed.

I found no humor in having to revive an organ that had previously been ready for climax.

My customer finished and left. Hugo entered once more while I was rinsing my mouth. He climbed onto my bed and reclined against the headboard. I turned to look at him.

"Good evening. Have you a—?"

He held up a yellow card. I forced a smile and crossed toward him, then his thumb slid to reveal a blue and a red beneath the yellow. I stumbled a step at the surprise. Once again, I tried to resume in character.

"My, my, you've bought all three. We're going to have a lot of fun."

"I think not." He tossed the cards beside him on the bed. "I don't take my pleasure in dingy attics. I would have you come to my home for a day."

I swept up the cards and put them in the pipe. *No refunds you obnoxious creep.*

I sat on the bed beside him. "Oh, I see. You must be Mr. Hugo."

His hand glided up my inner thigh. I wished he hadn't bought any cards so I could protest.

"Just Hugo, you sweet, defiant thing."

I stretched my lips in another false smile. "I was just giving him the same courtesy I give all my customers. The same courtesy I'm sure you would want for me to give to you."

"Yes, yes." He put his hand in my loincloth to grope my naked cock. "But you can't imagine my surprise. Mrs. Alita told me you were a fragile frightened little thing. How wrong she was."

I brought my hand to his cheek and caressed while opening my legs for him. "My spirit's not fragile, but my body is. And I truly was frightened, of being maimed or bruised, or choked. You are asking for a great deal of trust, and I don't know you."

"Show me your ass."

"Of course, darling." I lifted myself enough to shed the loincloth and then rolled so my back was

to him. He squeezed both buttocks with one mealy hand.

"Well you are very pretty. Young. Smooth." He fingered my crease. "There's a lot I could do with you."

"If I agree."

"Yes, if you agree. You know I'm paying 50 coin for you, correct?"

I leaned back to look at him. "I have all the money I need. I'd be gone already if not for my contract."

He cocked a brow. "Oh? When is it up?"

"July."

"I must have you before then. At least once, but preferably a few times. I don't think I'll ever tire of such supple flesh."

I rolled over to face him. My facade was lowered. Now was the time to be serious.

"What do you want to do to me?"

He licked his lips while looking down at my groin. "If I tell you, then you'll have no apprehension. That's half the fun."

"If you won't tell me, then you must consent to a chaperone."

"An audience? How interesting." He edged himself to the side of the bed to stand. "I accept your terms." He headed for the break in my curtain.

"You're going? You don't even want for me to suck you?"

"Completely impossible." He left.

I sat staring at the swinging curtain with my mouth agape. I wished to think about his words, but the next man entered, a young blond centerus who'd visited last month.

"Oh, you've come back!" I said, with a squeal of feigned joy.

14 The Freak

Richard will be pleased when he reads this chapter. I am not inclined to describe my day with Hugo in intricate detail. The memory sickens me and caused me to crawl into a bottle back then where I refused to take clients for four days.

I came to him with an attitude so vicious I could hardly find my character. First, those three cards he flashed in my room were given to him compliments of the inn. I received no payment for them, something I was unaware I might be subject to. Second, he'd robbed me of my day off. It wasn't discussed with me, simply announced. I'd agreed to an appointment at his home, hence it had to be on my next free day. Alita wouldn't consider making Hugo wait the week it would take for me to be free of appointments.

The chaperone was Gabin, who accepted the duty for two coin. I'd come to know him during my daily mealtimes and the two times he'd bought blue cards from me. He'd often ask me about my duties, how I felt about what I did, and how I got by. I had no difficulty unloading on him. He was a fine enough chaperone. Had it been Alita I would have felt inhibited.

Hugo's mansion was shared with his brother, with each of them taking residence half a year at a time. The décor bespoke wealth and normalcy, not at all what you'd expect in the home of a pervert. His true character was revealed in the lurid dungeon basement.

Gabin stayed to the side as I stripped and splayed my limbs in the shape of an x to be bound.

Here I'm sure you'll expect I describe the horrors that so sickened me about this date. In truth he did nothing more severe than what I enjoyed with Renherld. The difference was that I found no arousal.

Hugo himself was horrifying.

He stripped naked showing a middle-aged centerus body, fat-bellied, pale, and covered in coarse dark hair. This was not what disgusted me. I'd served miners who were far less shapely and still had an erection. It was his hideous groin. The sight put a look of revulsion in Gabin's face.

Hugo had no shaft to his member. I would say he'd been castrated, but he had normal testicles. Where a shaft should have been was a rim of flesh surrounding glistening red innards. The tube for his discharge would poke out of this when fluid needed to be expelled.

If he were a pathetic creature who'd suffered in a tragic accident, I could have had pity for him. This could not be further from the case. He was a monster who reveled in his monstrosity. He insisted that both Gabin and I look at his opening as though aroused by our disgust. Thrice white ejaculate came out of the hole while he beat me, making him yelp and quiver.

I wish not to disgust you, dear reader, but this was the reality of my experience. He was a cruel, grotesque thing who had me take part more in a hideous freak show rather than a sex act. My skin crawled. Bile rose in my throat. I couldn't find any arousal, even when he massaged the interior of my ass.

When my hours of torture were done, I still could not eat. Bugs squirmed beneath my skin. I couldn't get the vision of his glistening opening out

of my head. It plagued me for days, crippling my ability to function.

Not even a thousand coin was worth this.

"I will never take another appointment with that man," I said to Alita.

She fumed while walking away from table where I was trying to force down a meal. "A pity. He had nothing but good things to say about you."

Knowing that I pleased him only added to my disgust.

15 The Trainee

If one good thing could be said to have come out of my appointment with Hugo it was that my resolve was redoubled to escape at the end of my contract. I was on my final month and counted the days until my release.

On Tuesday I was organizing my belongings so they would fit in my pack. Gabin came up to my room. He sometimes visited when I was free to chat with me. I gave him a warm greeting.

"How goes it, Gabin?"

He sat on my bed with his back to me. "It goes, Kali."

He grew silent for a while. I continued working, not at all bothered by his presence. It was clear something was on his mind.

"So, I've been thinking about getting into the comfort game."

I froze. "You…really?"

He turned toward me and shrugged with one shoulder. "It's good money."

"That's true."

"I'm just getting by as a housekeeper. Seems like once I pay for my room here I've got barely a penny left." He snuffled. "I got to ask myself, is this all it's going to be for my life? I mean, you're going off to school after you're done. Going to make something of yourself. What am I ever going to do? If I could save up a thousand coin it'd be enough to open a grist mill or what have you. I could get a wife, a house, some children. I wouldn't end up dying alone in a shoebox like old Philipe."

"Hm."

"I'm not getting any younger, you know?"

"What about the stigma of being a rufine?"

He scowled. "Well, what about it? Let them gossip, I don't give a care. If I've got the money, a good business, a big house, I'll still land me a wife. People will have to get over it."

I pursed my lips. "Do you think you could take a centerus cock?"

He shot me a wry smile. "That's where you come in. I figure you can break me in and then it won't be so tough." He swallowed. "I'll buy a red card...though, I'll have to save up for it."

A jolt of stimulation went to my cock. I felt hunger build in my gaze. "You don't have to buy a card."

His face brightened. "Really?"

I licked my lip. "Yeah." My stuff was dumped onto the floor. "Come here."

His smile became sheepish. "Right now? I wasn't expecting right now."

"Are you sure this is what you want to do?"

He nodded. "I've thought a lot about it."

"So let me fuck you." I fluttered my lashes. "I'll be gentle."

He gave a nervous laugh.

I crawled beside him and glided my hands over his chest. My lips nipped his earlobe. "Don't back out."

"I ain't going to back out of anything." He grabbed me for a kiss.

We wrangled our tongues together, and I felt a heat more genuine than the kind I got from my customers. Gabin pulled off his tunic and crawled above me for more kissing. I wanted to allow

myself to melt beneath the sensual warmth of his body, but then remembered what we were doing.

"I should be on top."

"Should you?" He laughed.

I pushed him off and wriggled free from my loincloth. My cock pointed outward from my pelvis.

"You need to learn how to service the blue cards."

"Oh that? I don't need a lesson on that. How hard can it be?"

I crawled up to straddle his shoulders, my cock inches from his lips. "Show me."

His throat bobbed with a gulp. He moved his gaze from me to the head of my cock. One thick hand took hold of the root and the rest was pushed into his mouth.

The hot wet vise gave me a shiver. I hadn't even dreamed of enjoying the thing I so often gave during my time there.

"Lick the cap. Suck me."

Gabin followed my instruction beautifully. I couldn't help but pivot my hips as he went. He took me deep enough into his throat to gag, making my stomach flutter.

"That's nice. Suck harder. Move your head."

His mouth now massaged my length with intense suction. My eyes rolled back with the pleasure. How I would have loved to orgasm.

"Oh…yes." I rubbed my nipples with both hands. "Grab my ass."

He gripped me while still sucking. My sensitive bottom tingled beneath his strong fingers.

And then I forced myself to break free of him. He looked at me with wide eyes.

"I was getting close."

He nodded with realization.

"It rarely happens so fast. You need to be able to keep it up for fifteen minutes. Moaning helps them come faster. Pretend that you love their cock."

He smiled. "Wow."

I crept backwards on him to get to his groin. The outline of an erect organ tented the fabric of his pants. I unbuttoned them and pulled it free.

"Sucking me turned you on?"

"It's your moaning. The way you were squirming."

"Ah." I gave him a cursory stroke before pulling his pants off his hooves. "It's best not to come until your last customer for the night. You need to seem aroused with every client. Your satisfaction doesn't matter. Only there's."

He scoffed. "Damn."

I dug a gob of lubricant out of my canister and pushed back one of his thick thighs. His taut asshole, veiled with hair, came into view. All I did was touch it with my greased finger and he jerked the whole of his body away from me.

"Aw damn it, I can't do it! Not there."

I knelt in place staring at him. "What are you talking about?"

"I just can't do it. I don't want someone messing around with my ass."

"You barely let me touch you. This part feels good."

"The hell with that."

He grabbed me by my shoulders and maneuvered me beneath his large body once more. "I can't," he said with a kiss. "It's not going to happen."

I scowled. "Then you can't be a comfort worker. Most men come to me with red cards. It's what they want."

"You said it feels good? Well let me see." He claimed some lubricant on his finger and reached down to press it against my ass.

My scowl remained steadfast. "What are you doing?"

His finger slid over my ring. "This feels good?"

"You're not going to fuck me. I was supposed to fuck you."

His finger pried inside of me. "Come on."

I kicked his face with a hoof and sent him crashing off the bed. "You ass!" I snatched my loincloth and pushed my legs into it. "I get fucked day and night and on my one day off you think I'm going to give you a freebie?"

He climbed onto the edge of the bed rubbing his forehead. "No. I didn't mean for it to go that way. You just got me so worked up and—"

"Get out!"

"Don't be mad. I'm sorry."

"Get. Out."

He grumbled and found his pants. I watched him dress, seething with heaves of my chest. Then he was gone.

The fury would not leave me. He'd revived that excitement I'd lost for nearly a year by offering himself to me and then ruined it by turning into a typical selfish client. I wanted to cry.

This place had damaged me.

16 The Woods

The day of my liberation finally came. Alita no longer begrudged me my freedom, but rather insisted I vacate my room at once. Gabin truly did take up the trade, at least for oral work. He was the only replacement she had for me and was better than none.

I had no concern for my homelessness. In my bank account was 1,935 coin. Can you imagine such a sum? It was nearly double the amount I needed for two years tuition, and I could easily support myself on it until I moved to my dormitory. My life had renewed itself after a year of misery. I couldn't hold back my elation.

And, oh, dear reader, how wrong I was about my future. Forgive my foreboding, but I would not be honest to proceed as though everything went as it should.

I knew a twenty mile hike awaited me for my return trip so I pared down my belongings even more. My last two precious books were left behind in my room. I made space in my bag for my mountain of treasure, which was retrieved without difficulty at the Calico Trust.

Fifty coin makes a crown, and there is no larger denomination. I dared not get a bank order because I didn't know if it would be honored in Schaletar. Thus, I had 38 crowns and 35 coin to weigh down my backpack. I loathed the hike before me almost as much as the prospect of paying for a night at the inn. When I saw it was 2pm on the bank's clock I surrendered to the latter. I would not make it to my destination in time to get my carriage.

Before I attempted to find lodging I went to the winery and foolishly bought four bottles. I thought to stock up on my favorite varieties since I wouldn't be able to find them in Schaletar. The I realized I had no way to carry them. It is this purchase, in hindsight, that I regret most of all.

With my small tail figuratively tucked between my legs I went to Camille's counter and paid 5 pennies for a room. It was less appointed than my curtained quarters upstairs with only a bed and basket. The bathroom was shared with all the other rooms on the floor.

I ate some dinner I'd purchased at the restaurant. I drained one of my bottes. I played with my money. Then I went to sleep.

Sunlight woke me in the morning. It was low in the sky, making me leap up in a panic. My custom was to sleep until noon, but I had to hike 20 miles and catch a carriage at 1. I was determined to get out of Calico today.

I hastily packed, but had three bottles of wine left, none of which would fit in my back. My plan was to carry two bottles in my hands and abandon the third. Since they were all expensive, I uncorked the bottle I meant to leave and guzzled down half of it.

Stupid, stupid stupid.

By the time I got downstairs my vision was doubled and my gait unsteady. Camille yelled from the counter to ask if I was okay. I nudged my head toward her with a sneer since my hands were too burdened to wave her off.

I exited the inn and tried to orient myself. This was impossible because the world was spinning. I plotted the bank, winery, apothecary,

and restaurant in my head and was sure I knew which way to go.

You may remember that the inn was at the corner of the two main streets of Calico. I went down the wrong one. What's worse is that I trotted with as forth right a stride as I could manage. I refused to miss that carriage. I hurried my unsteady hooves down this incorrect path, taking no note of the wrong scenery around me.

I was a faun in a centerus town. I still stood out as much as I ever did, likely more so for I was laden with a heavy pack and had two bottles of wine in my hands. The wine gave any onlooker a clue to why my step was unbalanced. Most of the men knew I'd been the town's comfort worker and could guess I was hauling a pack because I was at the end of my contract and leaving. They could surmise I likely had a lot of money. I could not have made more of a target of myself if I tried. I mention this only because it might help me fathom what happened later.

I reached the end of the street. The paving turned to dirt. The houses and businesses had long since ended. Before me was forest framed by distant mountains.

I realized I'd gone the wrong way, but somehow thought I could skirt around the edge of town to make my way back. I didn't wish to retrace my steps as I'd walked a good half hour. A shortcut was ideal if I was still going to catch my carriage.

I went left, or so I thought. The forest that had been in front of me soon consumed me. Still I continued on, thinking I knew the way. By gods I was so terribly drunk.

Thud. I remember the sound. There was no pain, however. Only instant darkness.

When I woke it was dark outside. My pack was gone. My two bottles were shattered on the ground. The back of my head throbbed with furious pain.

Oh, dear reader, I can't describe my horror. My disbelief. My madness which verged on thoughts of suicide. It was gone. All gone. Everything I'd worked for the past year, everything I owned except a tunic and a loincloth. I'd been destroyed in one fragile instant.

I could not cry, nor move. The truth of the horror was more than my mind could accept. To add insult to my trauma, I was nauseous and dizzy. Once I'd summoned the power to stand I could barely manage it. I leaned against a tree in the dark still too overwhelmed to fathom my lot.

Tears came some time later. The agonizing emotion made my parched throat ache. I began to wander the woods in the moonlight looking for a source of water. All the wretchedness of my lot could be put aside until my thirst was quenched.

I wandered for hours.

When daylight came I managed to find a brook, and the lift from that small triumph allowed me to assess my situation.

I refused to go back to the inn. *No, damn it!* I'd sooner die than start over. That place was where my spirit had been broken.

I had nothing back in Schaletar, and not even the means to pay for my travel back there. Oh gods, what a pitiful state I was in. I pondered briefly the idea of working at least a day in the inn just to get my fare before talking myself out of it. Alita would force me into another wretched year contract by keeping my money hostage.

It struck me that I didn't know how to get back to Calico even if I wished. My next goal was finding a vista so I could get my bearings. (Though I had no idea what I would do after that.) I followed the brook for miles, presuming it would lead to a higher source. If nothing else, I kept precious water near me.

The sun set on the first day of my disaster. I curled myself at the base of an oak and shivered to sleep. The next morning I was still devastated, but somehow filled with new perspective. It had happened. Nothing could change it. Thinking of all the cocks I sucked and all the men I let use me was self-defeating. What was done was done.

And I was ravenously hungry. All I could do was find edible weeds and the odd berry as I walked. I knew not how long I'd have to subsist this way. No opportunity for sustenance was overlooked, even bird's eggs.

I finally found the source that fed the brook near dusk. Now my legs ached, but the back of my head no longer throbbed. I had a formidable lump between my horns. The criminal must have bashed me with a vertical strike to get between them.

The brook was fed by a pond at the base of a sheer rock mountainside. A waterfall fed the pond. I was now at the end of my trail, and night approached. I loathed the idea of sleeping exposed to the elements once more.

Behind the waterfall was a cave. I skirted the rock and splashed through the veil of water to inspect it. It was a deep crevice with dim light pouring in from its other side. I went in far enough to escape the wetness and then arranged some moss for my bed. I had blocked the wind on both sides

and was grateful for the shelter. I fell into a deep sleep.

Light brightened every inch of my crevice the next…well, not morning. The low sun told me I'd slept until noon again. The rest revived me.

I looked toward the opposite side from where I'd entered. I could now see that the exit was quite distant. With the only other option being an icy splash beneath the waterfall again I crawled toward the far off light. In a while I was able to walk upright. It took me close to an hour to reach the exit of the cave. This was a shock. I realized I'd gone underneath the mountains.

I emerged on a hillside that sloped down into thin woods. A line of smoke came from a camp a mile off. Dear reader, I was so hungry by now I was ready to beg or sell myself for some food. Being willing to do so much for a meal is almost liberating. I trotted towards the camp with renewed gusto.

Then I slowed when I got close. I could hear their voices and smell their food. The scents were strange, and so were their accents. It took my ears a while to start making out their words. I realized a woman was among them and was encouraged. Thieves and ruffians don't have women in their gangs.

The group of five figures were walled on two sides by closed wagons. I heard the grunts of horses near them. They sat on toppled logs close to a fire. I approached gingerly. They appeared to be centeri because I did not see horns.

One of them, a lean man in his fifties, caught sight of me. He bumped the arm of the man beside him.

"Richard, look!"

The man, Richard (how it delights me to introduce him) turned his body to look at me. His eyes widened. His jaw fell open. I heard him gasp.

I presumed it was because of my loincloth. It sickened me that I'd been robbed of my pants. I brought the story of my misfortune to the front of my mind to explain my indecency.

"Hello," Richard said softly, while rising so carefully it put a stitch in my brow. "Don't be afraid." He gestured with one gentle hand. "No one's going to hurt you."

Now the entire group stared at me. I couldn't fathom the wonder on their face. Richard climbed over the log to move toward me. I gasped and staggered back. This was no centerus. He had legs that bent at an angle, and hooves clad in leather that pointed out like the feet of a duck.

He halted and panic flashed on his regal face. "No, no. Don't run away, sweetness. Please don't."

A giant man thrice the size of Richard bolted up from his log and went into a wagon. I managed to hold my ground.

"What are you?" I said.

"What are we?" the only woman among them said. "What the hell are you? Richard, you said they'd have horse legs, and you didn't say anything about horns."

"So what," Richard said to her out of the side of his mouth. "Isn't this even better? It's stunning."

I narrowed my eyes at being called an it. "I'm a faun."

"A faun, my God." Richard continued smiling at me. "Come here, won't you? What's your name?"

The creatures, whatever they were, appeared friendly, and I was too hungry to stand on ceremony. I lifted a hoof to walk towards them.

A net closed over me. I screamed and struggled with my arms and legs to get free. The large man who'd gone into the wagon had circled behind me. He bunched up the net in his fist and held me aloft with one thick arm.

"There! I caught it!"

The woman clapped her hands and gave a squeal of glee.

Richard hopped up and ran to me. "Damn it, Callum! He was coming over to sit with us."

I ceased floundering once I realized I had an advocate.

"Yeah," Callum said with a sneer beneath his waxed mustache. "Then he gets startled and runs away. When are we ever going to see another one of these fucking things?" He carried me to the back of one of the wagons. To my horror, it was a cage. "I'm putting him in Duncan's cage."

Richard grabbed his arm and was pulled along with us. "No, damn it. Let me talk to him! I don't want a prisoner."

Callum dumped me into the cage and locked it. I worked my way out of the net with my heart thundering.

Callum, bald except for his unibrow and mustache and standing head and a half taller than Richard, jabbed a gigantic finger into his face. "You talk to it. You make sure it stays. You let it get away and we're back in the same fucking shit again. I don't care if it's a fucking prisoner or not."

Richard knocked the finger out of his face. "I think you're forgetting who's in charge here."

"And you're forgetting who fucked us all up in Brixberry!" Callum scoffed and stomped away. "We got it, don't we? Who gives a fuck if we hurt its feelings."

Richard walked over to my cage. "I care," he said, looking where Callum had gone, but speaking to me. He faced me with gentle blue eyes. The wagon was on high wheels so I only saw him from the chest up where I crouched in the cage.

Even back then I noticed how his fine striped linen shirt was stuffed by the definition of his chest. The giant man had been grotesquely muscled, but Richard was of a lovely proportionate build. His face, smooth except for a pointed goatee, was wide at the jaw and framed with dense black locks of hair. I'll never forget this, my first impression of him. The man was stunning.

"What did you say your name was?" Richard said in dulcet tones meant to be calming.

"Kali." I spat the word back to him.

"I'm sorry, Kali. As you can see, I'm not entirely in control of my troupe. I'd get rid of that oaf in a heartbeat if he wasn't so effective at managing rowdy crowds."

I glared at him. He still smiled, oozing charm that could not be stifled by my outrage.

"We're in a bit of a pickle, Kali."

"So am I."

"I'm going to get you free. But hear me out first. Is that fair enough?"

I gave a solitary nod.

"See, around here there's stories of creatures with the bodies of men and the legs and tails of horses."

"The centeri." I was growing impatient.

"Yes, the centeri, or centaurs or what have you. We're a traveling carnival. Callum's my strong man." He pointed to the others still sitting around the fire, and partially in my view. His finger fixed on the woman. "Maisie is our fortune teller, also my wife." He pointed to a man who looked like a teenager. "Fergus there is our acrobat and juggler, quite good at both, but mute as the come." He pointed the older man who'd alerted him to me. This one had shaved the sides of his graying brown hair. (I would later learn he was trying to imitate the mane of a horse.) "Duncan's Fergus' father. He…well I don't know quite what he does anymore. I'm thinking he'll make a sad clown for us. But, anyway I'm Richard, carnival master and grand orator of the works of Marquis Rye. My verses will make your toes curl. If you had toes that is." He took a bow. "At your service."

"Service me by getting me out of this cage."

Richard widened his lips in a smile while looking up and down at me. He spoke without the facade of the great carnival master he'd briefly assumed. "Where did you come from?"

"I can show you, if you let me out."

He wet his lips in his mouth. "If I let you get away, I might be hanged in Brixberry. The others too."

I pretended I didn't care.

"We've been perpetuating a bit of a fraud, I'm afraid. Completely harmless, entertainment is entertainment and I say if a crowd oos and ahhs I've done my job right. But still, we had our Duncan pretending to be a centerus. We put a costume on him. Furred leg wraps, hooves, a long horse's tail. He was the gem of our carnival. Everyone wanted to see him."

"How did you manage the shape of the legs?"

His nose lifted toward me. "What's that?"

"The centeri have legs like mine, except thicker. Your legs are straight with a weird sharp bend."

"Oh, right. So they're like the back legs of horses I imagine." He squinted at me. "So there really are centeri, huh?" His face returned to normal. "Oh, what am I saying? You're real aren't you? There's probably lots of half human half animal creatures on the other side of the death cliffs."

"Half what?"

"Human. That's what we are. So, anyway—"

"How many human are there? How did we not know you existed?"

He balked. "Well, I could ask the same of your kind. I've never heard of fauns! I still can't believe you're really in front of me. Every time I blink I think you're going to disappear." He laughed. "We've scarcely even heard of centeri. There was tell of an actual centerus some hundred years ago. His skeleton is in the king's museum. I was never sure it was real, but I'd hoped. It did capture folk's imagination, and we've got this black space on our maps that not even the stoutest sailing ship can get round to." He gestured towards the mountains. "Who knows what lies beyond it? But to answer your question, no one knew Duncan's legs weren't right for a centerus. No one's ever seen one, and precious few have even seen the supposed skeleton. They wanted to believe a centerus lived among us and Duncan provided that fantasy."

"Hm."

"But a few days ago in Brixberry he didn't tie his leg wrap right. He was in a mood, you see. Didn't want to bother. And the fur part slipped down showing ordinary hairy man-leg. The crowd jeered at us and threw turnips. We had to pack-up and make a fast getaway. But some bastard called the magistrate on us. We were stopped at the city gates and forced to give up all the money we'd made, in Brixberry or otherwise. Even then the magistrate's men were crowding around us ordering that we turn back. I knew there was a hanging in our future, so I proffered up a lie to get us free. I said we had a real centerus, but he had to go home for a visit to his family. That's why Duncan was filling in. I said if he let us go I'd be back in a week with a real centerus for everyone to see. I tell you, men are so enchanted with the thought of seeing a fantasy creature they'll believe most anything. He agreed to let us go on the condition we come back in seven days with a real centerus. If not we'd be hunted down as criminals. He was going to inform the earl about our fraudulent troupe and the earl would inform the king and we'd be posted all over as wanted men."

My stare at him went dry. "I'm not a centerus."

He threw up his hands joyfully. "You're even better than one! A creature no one's even heard of. Think how it will excite the imagination! How it will open doors of possibility for what's out there."

I was still dry. "You promised the magistrate you'd bring back a real centerus."

"Indeed. And now I shall say our loyal friend and worker could not return due to his family

troubles. He lamented abandoning us, so found an even rarer creature to send in his place. Kali, the magical, mystical faun!"

"I am neither of those things."

"You look truer than anything I could sew together. A squeeze of your hooves, a tug of your cute little tail, at look at those backwards bending legs, they'll have no doubt you're genuine."

"My legs bend correctly."

"You'll be the instant gem of our carnival. Better than a centerus—I already had one of those. You're something people will have to see to believe. A mystical, magical faun from the land of…what land?"

"Schaletar."

"Oh, that sounds fantastical." His blue eyes gleamed at me. "Kali, the mystical faun from magical realm of Schaletar."

"There is nothing even remotely magical about my town."

Richard took a moment to collect himself. His face still brimmed with excitement. "Please join my troupe. The pay is good. I'll give you a room right in my own private wagon. All you'll have to do is pose in this cage while people look at you. You'll travel throughout the country. You'll have good friends. Good fun. Grand excitement. I swear to you, we're not terrible people. Even Callum for all his lummoxry."

I was sold, but I didn't let it read on my face. What other options had I? This wondrous opportunity had landed in the midst of my devastation, pulling me out of it on the wings of this charming angelic man. I could only hope this would prove my salvation and not be another miserable job as I'd had with Mrs. Alita. If nothing

else, it was a chance to earn money and begin again far removed from the land of my destruction.

He reached into my cage and clasped my leg. "Please, Kali. I swear you won't regret it." He began tapping and tugging my hoof. "I know not who you've got waiting for you, or what obligations you have in Schaletar. I beg you to put it all aside at least long enough for us to get you back to Brixberry. If you really must settle things we'll take you back here afterwards. I give you my solemn word on that—and you'll come to realize I never break my word."

I let him stew a moment and then lifted my nose in the air. "I'll think about it."

Richard's brow quivered.

"But not on an empty stomach."

He brightened. "Of course, of course, we've got rat and turnip stew." His white-toothed grin reappeared. "The turnips are courtesy of the disgruntled rabble of Brixberry. Maisie said damn if she would pass up a chance to collect a bushel of free turnips."

"I don't eat rats."

He frowned. "One mustn't be picky on the road. I could have told you it was chicken and you wouldn't have known the difference."

"I don't eat the flesh of any animal. I'm not a wolf or a raven. It's obscene to me that civilized creatures would kill animals to feed on them. Just turnips will do."

"Oh, I see. This is because you're half animal yourself."

I glowered at him.

He gave me an infernally charming smile to erase my ire.

"And let me out of this cage."

Richard dropped to his knees and raised prayerful hands toward me. "If you run away, we'll be ruined and probably hanged. Have mercy for my position!"

I met his glimmering eyes. "I won't run away. You'll come to learn that I also never break my word."

Richard stared at me a moment, then got up slowly. He lifted the latch securing the door (which I now realized I could have lifted myself). His strong arm was offered to help me down. I accepted it and lowered beside him. He was several inches taller than me.

"Don't be offended, but you are beautiful, no matter what manner of creature you are."

I let one side of my mouth curl toward a smile. "Why would that offend me?"

He bowed as though bested and walked me to the rest of the gathering.

17 Richard

Richard mentioned that I never described myself in my adulthood. I would think a portrait of me will be on the cover of this book, perhaps a recreation of the lovely though scandalous poster of me crouching naked in the woods which was used on the side of the wagon to promote me. Still, I shall not be remiss.

I never got as tall as Mr. Renherld, but I did manage to be taller than most faun women. I matched the height of Richard's wife, who was the second shortest of our troupe topping only the small Fergus (who was actually close to the age of 30 when I met him).

I wore my straight white hair long and have the large curling horns of a ram. My face is pretty, either by the standard of a man or a woman, with pink lips and big eyes with dense lashes. I was lovely enough to entrance every patron who sought me at Alita's inn, and likely managed an income greater than other comfort workers.

I have what might be considered human legs to my knees, and the legs of a ram below this with broad cleft hooves and fur above them somewhat darker than the hair on my head. I was of slender build, with some musculature but none that could compete with my dear Richard's.

***

I ate roasted turnips alone on the log seat as four of them broke camp, and Callum stood guard near me. Duncan and Fergus entered one of the wagons. Maisie entered the other. Richard fussed at the doorway of his and Maisie's wagon and then beckoned.

Within was a table against one wall with a built in bench seat and chairs on the other side. The middle of the berth was piled high with leather-covered chests leaving only enough room to walk to either the table or the other side of the wagon which held a curtained off bed that could fit two.

Maisie was on this bed in a nightgown brushing long ringlets of blonde hair before a mirror. She looked far too young to be the bride of Richard, who was perhaps 30. But then, I was probably the same age as her. My time as a prostitute had made me worldly beyond my years.

In the narrow walking area before the crates was a cushion which I presumed had come from the long bench behind the table. Richard had added a pillow to this to create a mattress for me. A wool blanket was folded on the cushions.

"Here we are," he said while inviting me in. "That should do for tonight. I'll rearrange things when we've more time."

"It's fine, thank you."

I climbed in, closed the door, and settled myself on the makeshift bed. Richard went to the other bed and pulled the curtain closed.

"Is he going to live with us permanently?" Maisie said.

I heard Richard shuffling. "For the time being."

"What does that mean? Is he going to be living with us or not?"

"Well I can't put him in Duncan's wagon. Just go to sleep."

"But it will be so crowded. We need another wagon. It should only be two for each one."

"I can't exactly be buying wagons now can I?"

"But when, then? I don't want to live like this. How can I walk in and out? What if I have to go pee?"

I grumbled. I was exhausted and grateful for some indoor comforts. How long did she intend to whine?

"We'll rearrange things later. Maybe get the crates latched to the top."

"How will I get my things if the crates are on top!"

"I'll fetch them for you, Maisie. For goodness sakes go to sleep."

"Well I don't like this and I'm not going to stand for it for very long."

"Noted! Now sleep."

"Why can't he stay in the cage?"

"Oh, Maisie, my God. This creature is saving all our lives! Can't you look at the big picture?"

She scoffed, but then was mercifully silent. I fell into a deep sleep.

I woke in the dead of night a few hours later. Maisie was working her bare feet carefully around my body to make it to the door. She smiled at me when I looked at her.

"I have to pee."

"Oh, sorry." I rolled to her room.

When she opened the door, there was an explosion of noise from a pile of bells attached to it. Maisie nearly fell down the steps in fright.

"Who did this!" she cried, once outside.

I heard the thumping feet of Callum. "What! What! He trying to get away?"

"No, you idiot, I'm going to pee. Why did you put all the damn—"

"I won't let him sneak away in the middle of the night!"

The door closed and their voices became muted.

Richard groaned from his curtained bed. "Ah, who needs sleep anyway?"

I concentrated on the starlight filtering through two windows to see if he'd say anything more.

"You still there, Kali?"

"Yes."

"Good. Try to get some sleep."

"I was trying."

Richard laughed. "So was I, my pet. So was I."

His pet? I wished to grow offended, but enjoyed him giving me a nickname so early in our acquaintance. I would tolerate pet, so long as he didn't mean it literally.

The bells exploded once more just as I was falling back to sleep. Maisie stepped on my hoof while climbing back in. I tried to give her room. Then I realized she wasn't moving off my cushion. I looked at her.

"Are you really half sheep?"

My brows pulled together. "Half what?"

She reached down and tugged my horn. I tolerated this with a scowl. Then she pulled the blanket off my legs and worked her fingers through my fur.

"Who would believe it? We've got a real mystical animal man." She met my eyes. "And you're so handsome. You look like a beautiful fairy."

I blinked at her in the dimness, not knowing what to say.

"Are we ugly to you?" Her voice became hushed.

"No."

"What about me? Do you think I'm pretty?"

"What are you doing Maisie?" Richard said from the bed.

"I'm just making sure it's real!"

"Let him sleep."

She glowered in his direction, then turned to smile at me. Her hand ran over my furry shin.

"Well, goodnight magical faun."

"Goodnight."

She disappeared behind her curtain. I was too tired to give the exchange much thought.

In the morning Richard invited me to sit beside him outside the wagon in the driver's seat. Callum drove the other wagon behind us.

"Thank you for not running away." He flashed a brief smile before focusing on the downward trailing road.

"You're welcome."

"I'd like for you to become a proper member of our troupe. I know you haven't said yes yet. Still, I'm hopeful. You're the once in a lifetime attraction that could get us performing for the king." He sighed at the thought. "Why don't you tell me about you? Give me some idea of what it would take to convince you to stay."

I stared outward at the rolling pasture dotted with bright green trees below us. To convey my desperate situation would have been foolhardy. I twisted my lips while thinking of what to say.

"You were more likely to meet a centeri where you were camped. It's their land on the other

side of the mountains, the death cliffs as you called them. Though the nearest centeri village is far from where I passed through the mountain. I was working for the centeri, and my contract had ended. Then I tried to head back home and got lost. I'd been hiking two days when I came to your camp."

"What do you mean by passed through the mountain?"

"There was a crevice through a waterfall, blocked by a tree on the other side."

"My word. So if you show me this crevice I could find a real centerus to work for me?"

"You would have to go through and then hike through the forest a good ways before you found their village."

He nodded. "That's a consideration for the future. You could find this passage again, right?"

"It was just up the hill from your camp."

"My, my." He wet his lips. "What other manner of creature is beyond that mountain?"

"I only know of fauns and centeri. There are carnivals on my side who would be glad to have one of you as an exhibit."

He swung back his head and laughed. "Imagine that! So it's civilized then, with money and businesses and traveling carnivals and all that?"

I considered a moment. "I'd taken a job in a centeri village to save money so I could pay for the education I needed to become a teacher."

"Ah yes. So extremely civilized, with colleges and so forth."

"Finishing schools we called them."

"So your dream is to become a teacher?"

I watched the dirt road moving beneath us. "To call it a dream would be an exaggeration. I aspired to be an educated professional. Teaching

was something that appeared to suit me since I enjoyed my studies and was an avid reader."

"Are you now? Do you know the works of Marquis Nye?"

"I've never heard of him."

"Where do you run, my softest eyes, in the trees and below what lies, the tender coiling of the wind, the branches sharp to tear you."

His breathless poem recital caused a crackle at the base of my scalp which scattered into euphoric tingles through my body. My lips parted and I was mesmerized. If I had toes I certain they would have curled. I tried to swallow this down and find some composure.

"Is the night not a spear, a lure to those found most dear, a terror for that we cannot see, in the blinding shroud we always fail."

Richard's eyes rolled back, and he gave a shudder with his entire body. "Oh, my sweet Kali. I can't have you posturing in a cage like a dumb animal. You need to come onto the stage with me. What voice and carriage you have."

I felt my face grow warm.

"You're too good to be a teacher," he continued. "Be a star in my carnival. Who wants to deal with mischievous brats, anyway?"

"I'll think about it."

"And I'll convince you." He spoke with certainty. "I could swear God himself sent you. We were at our darkest hour, Kali. We lost every pence of our money. They were going to ban us throughout the country—hunt us even. Then suddenly you appeared. Now everything's good again."

Tears brimmed in my eyes because I felt the same about him. I had lost everything, and then this handsome man appeared.

"Tell me about this carnival," I said once my emotion had dissipated. "How did you come to lead it?"

"Ah, well, when I was but a stripling lad of eight a carnival far bigger than this filled the square of my hometown with caged animals, magicians, jugglers, and fire-spitters. My mother was raising me with my six brothers and sisters all alone and had no money to spare for a ticket. So I sneaked under the fabric of a tent and watched all the majesty of their performances. I did so every day they were in town, never once losing my sense of awe. Then when they were breaking down their tents, I ran to the carnival master asking to work for him. I claimed I was an orphan, a lowly street urchin with no family. He said they'd take me along to clean the animal cages, but for no pay, only a place to sleep and my bread. I eagerly accepted."

"What did your mother say?"

"I thought she'd be glad to get rid of me. There were too many mouths to feed in our home. Not enough space for all of us. But no, she chased the carnival to the next town to fetch me, missing a day of work and being forced to buy a ride on a coach."

I clucked my tongue.

"I had a fury unleashed on me by both my mother and the carnival master. But I was a clever boy, even then. I told my mother this was my dream, my hope for a better life, and I told the carnival master to buy me from her. He offered thirty pounds for me, and not a pence more. That was a princely sum in my family, enough to take us

out of debt and buy a whole pig for the larder. I saw her thinking about it and pushed her over the edge by reminding her she'd see me every year when the carnival returned to town. She took the money and then asked the carnival master to promise he'd take good care of me. He swore to her he would treat me like his very own son. She left me with tears in her eyes. That's when I realized how callous I'd been to run away with no regard for her. My mother truly loved me; she just hadn't much time to show it with her long hours of labor and five other children."

"I'm glad you understood that."

"And to his credit, Jules, the carnival master, did treat me as his own. Not at first. He had me running ragged cleaning animal shit and fetching things for the performers. I had to prove my worth to him a good few months before he took a shine to me. Then he tried to find a gimmick for me because all the performers from the acrobats to the clowns worked multiple jobs. So Richard the cage-cleaner could also be Richard the clown. But this was beneath my talent. I fancied myself a great actor, not a painted ponce. I advanced from common clown to sad clown and then pauper clown. I preferred the pitiful characters where I could add drama and make the audience coo mournfully at me. The more reaction I managed to get the better I would perform. I was truly a natural. Now, I couldn't do flips, never learned to juggle, would break my neck on the stilts, and was lousy with trained animals, but my talent was that of an actor, a fine one, a magnificent one, and that's what launched me into fame. When I was ten, Jules claimed I was only eight, and I would recite the full thirty verses of Dominicus. It was a spectacle to see

a child orate such a lengthy piece, but the story itself mesmerized them. I acted out each character, heightened every emotion, gesticulated my whole body even dropping to my knees in the beggar's scene. Hundreds of massive eyes would be fixed on me. I had them riveted. And when I was done, they launched to their feet to applaud me."

"Wow. This at only ten."

"In the business I'm what you call a natural. And that was good, because as I said, I was lousy at all the other gimmicks."

"Did your mother come to approve?"

Richard's face beamed with excitement. "Oh, that's the best part. I nearly forgot. We didn't make it back to Dorsky—that's my hometown—until two years later. I didn't even recognize my town square after seeing so many others. I put on my great oration of Dominicus without realizing my own family watched in the audience. Jules had let them in for free. My mother caught me back stage, cheering and crying. She squeezed me in her arms and painted me with kisses. I'd just proven she'd made the right decision to let me go." He took a deep breath. "It was a magnificent reunion. And she was doing better by then. Every time I came home her situation improved. She got a new husband, a provider who was good to my siblings."

"That's lovely."

"Yes, I kept up the Dominicus performance until I looked too old to pass as a little kid. Jules kept me in his wagon and had a full library built into a wall. He pointed out books with poems or plays I could recite. This was my education. I read those hundred books ragged. Every story I considered performing. Sometimes I'd start reading aloud without realizing it and Jules would shush me

from his bed. I picked the most famous, most sensational pieces to perform. In my teens I did two orations a night, not only because the crowds adored me, but because we could shut off all the lamps except for the one pointed at me and change the set for the next act."

"How long did this continue?"

He shrugged. "Until I was a man. Until Jules became feeble, and I had to step in as his mouthpiece more often than not. The acrobats were from Zurrucksor, that's a country where thievery is an obligation whenever a person has a chance. They were constant trouble, breeding discontent throughout the troupe, but Jules kept them on because the rigging for their act had been so expensive. That was a mistake. Then he mentioned he would retire soon. The acrobats didn't want me in charge because they knew I'd kick them out. Other performers, the fire-eater, the juggler, the animal trainer, they left one by one when they got tired out. Our bear and two ponies died. Ticket sales began to dwindle. We had to travel further out of the cities to amaze people, and those crowds were poor." He glanced at me. "I guess this is all a long way of saying we were put out of business. Jules went home and found an old widow to marry. The acrobats stole our mules and the rigging for their platforms in the night and fled back to Zurrucksor. Three clowns who shared a wagon sold it, and I followed suit, selling our large tent and throwing away the bulky stage dressings. I spoke of a smaller carnival, with only two or three wagons, where costs could be kept low and profits high. Duncan and Fergus were the first to join. Maisie was a local girl in our last venue who made time with me. She begged me to take her, but her father

wouldn't abide it unless I married her. That seemed a good idea at the time—this was four years ago mind you. Callum was picked up along the way since we needed a man to help control the rowdy crowds."

"So you've a more humble carnival now."

"Not humble at all. We put on a show just as marvelous as Jule's big tent, but with efficiency and fewer moving parts. The crowds would team us because we had a centerus. That got them there, and the rest of the show would dazzle them. You see, even though I couldn't master any gimmicks under Jules, I came up with the most sensational one for my own show. We make as much as Jules did with his massive caravan, and with only our two wagons." He snuffled. "It's just a shame we were caught. The rewards for the gamble were incredible, but the risk was just as incredible. Fraudsters are hanged in this country."

My lips screwed to the side. "That seems overly severe."

He turned up one hand.

"It's good you no longer have to deceive people."

Richard looked at me. "Are you saying you'll stay, Kali?"

I nodded sideways to give him a maybe. "Right now I believe I'll stay. That may change as I come to know more."

Richard took my hand. "Please stay. God, what will I do if I don't have you?"

His hand was warm and tingly over mine. I wanted to say I'd stay for his sake, because he was likeable. This seemed too forward. The man was married. Even if I'd probably betrayed a hundred wives as a whore, it was not in my nature to be so

devious. I wished to move past my transgressions at Alita's inn.

We took a break at midday where I shared bread with the others while seated on the grass. Then we rode until dusk and made another camp with another fire. I had roasted turnips and wild mushrooms. The rest ate rat stew.

"So is he with us?" Callum asked Richard over their steaming bowls.

"He's with us for now. Let's not make him change his mind."

Fergus beamed a smile at me and gave a playful shove to my shoulder. I smiled back, then looked at Duncan for further confirmation. The older man stayed fixed on his stew.

"Are we going to rearrange the wagon for him tonight?" Maisie said.

Richard shook his head. "Let's get settled somewhere for a while, dear. We're all tired."

"But it's too crowded."

"Please, Maisie."

"Come sleep in our wagon if it's too tight for you," Callum said, scooping an ample bite of stew in his mouth. "There's room."

Richard shot him a look of pure hatred. I got a shiver down my spine.

Maisie threw up her hands. "Oh forget it. I guess we'll just keep being uncomfortable."

Fergus started making symbols with his hands. It appeared to be a language.

"No," Richard said to him. "We don't have two pence to rub together."

I blinked.

"What did he say?" Maisie parried her head between them. "Did he say we should get another wagon?"

"How can we even discuss that right now?" Richard said.

Callum gestured to me. "Because you've got this deer-boy or sheep-boy or whatever now. The crowds are going to pile on us more than ever. There will be plenty enough to buy another wagon."

Richard's eyes narrowed. "Oh? And you're up on the price of wagons?"

"We need another space." Callum's voice rose.

"Why?" Richard said. "There's three people in your wagon and three in mine."

"Because you should stop being so fucking cheap, that's why."

"I can't spend money I don't have! We're penniless."

"Bah." He climbed up and stomped off to his wagon. A candle light came on in one window.

The rest ate in silence a while.

"We doing another show in Brixberry?" Duncan said.

"I don't know. We'll see what happens."

Duncan snuffled loudly as though making a challenge. "Well what do you have planned for me? I got a right to know."

Richard looked at him. "What would you like to do, Duncan?"

The man's face reddened. "I told you when I came into this I don't got no talents. I was spose to just be your horse-man."

Richard's blue eyes flickered in the fire-light at him. "You could be a rusher, but it won't be the same pay."

Duncan's lower lip quivered with fury. "What do I got to do to keep my wages?"

"Do a clown act with Callum."

Duncan looked away. "And I'm the clown, is that it?"

Richard's voice remained steady. "Unless you have a better idea."

He bolted upright and tromped to his wagon, slamming the door behind him. Fergus said something with his hands.

"There's nothing I can do about that. Jules had him shoveling bear shit for five years. You'd think he could handle clown work."

Fergus shrugged, gathered the dirty bowls of the other two men, and followed his father into the wagon.

I waited a beat for the tension to dissipate in the air, and then said, "How do you understand what he's saying?"

"Fergus and I have known each other for twenty years."

I balked.

"He's thirty years old, Kali."

"I thought he was a teenager."

"Everyone does," Maisie said. "I'm the only young one here. I'm twenty years old."

This surprised me, but with less power as the revelation about Fergus. I'd thought she was seventeen.

"How old are you, Kali? My guess is the same as Maisie."

"I'll be twenty this year."

Maisie's jaw fell open. "So you're younger than me? But I liked being the youngest."

Richard pulled her close to kiss her forehead. "We all have to get old, my dear."

"I am not old!"

With that I settled into the wagon with them for my second night with the carnival.

18 Maisie

Again, Maisie bumped me to get to the door. This time she didn't exit. She crouched beside me and touched my hair. I sat up to escape her hand.

"So we're the same age." She spoke at a whisper.

"Yes."

"Richard's not. He's old as dirt."

"He doesn't seem old."

"Oh, but he's thirty. That's terribly old."

"Hm."

"Do you think I'm pretty, Kali?"

"Stop doing this."

She recoiled as though stricken. "Doing what?"

"You're flirting with me."

Her lips bunched. "I haven't done anything."

"But what do you mean to do?"

She lifted her nose. "Who says I mean to do anything?"

"I won't betray Richard."

She turned away. "He's not a good man. He can't even give me a baby, and he's cross with me."

"That's between you and him. Please go back to bed."

She shoved herself to her feet. "I'm not going to bed. I have to pee." Her pale hand flung open the door (this time without any bells) and she left.

I heard Richard shifting. He pulled back the curtain and looked at me. My lips parted.

"She's a handful," he said, looking defeated.

"I don't want to cause trouble between you."

"Trust me. She causes all the trouble herself." He shook his head. "I don't know why I can't keep her. It wasn't true what she said. Well, the part about me being cross with her, anyway."

I swallowed. I hadn't been sure if he heard us. "There's nothing I can say. I have no experience with this sort of thing."

He blinked. "I'm not asking for you to fix my marriage. Just keep rebuffing her."

"Of course."

He forced a smile and let the curtain fall closed. The door blasted open and Maisie stomped on my legs to get back to her bed.

She was right. We needed another wagon.

19 The Magistrate

Richard had us stop the wagons when a village appeared several miles in front of us.

He tipped his nose at it. "That's Brixberry."

He climbed down and I followed him to the wagon's door. Maisie opened it looking annoyed.

"Go to Duncan's wagon."

She sneered. "What? Why would I?"

Richard looked away and chewed his lower lip. "I'm thinking we better not all go in. Just me and Kali."

"Why!"

"Because they might still want to hang us, even after I show them a faun."

She sealed her lips.

Richard walked her to Duncan's wagon. The five carnival members had a meeting beside it. Richard explained his fear.

"So we camp here until we get word from you?" Callum said.

Richard chewed his lip again. "Yeah. I'll see if I can ride back and let you know if everything goes well. Give me two days."

"Two days!" Duncan said.

"Two days. If you don't hear from me by then assume the worse and get away from the town."

"The worse being that they hanged you," Callum said.

Richard nodded. "Does everyone understand?"

Maisie threw up her hands with sound of aggravation. "Fine! Let me get some stuff out of our wagon then."

Things were sorted with her, and then Richard and I climbed back into the driver's seat. He shook the reins for our set of horses to continue.

"Why are you having misgivings now? You seemed so confident before."

I heard him swallow. "One never knows what will happen. The chief magistrate here is crooked."

What if they hang you, Richard? What will become of your wife?

I had more sense than to ask. There was less risk on my end. I'd committed no fraud and was a mystical beast to these people. My only worry was for Richard's sake.

The town was surrounded by a stone wall with a single iron gate allowing people to enter or exit. I'd never seen such an enclosure. What were they guarding against? Monsters?

Two magistrates with swords stood inside the railings. Richard climbed down, spoke to them, pointed at me, and the gate was opened.

Within the wall was a dense village teaming with humans in ragged clothes. Homes were built against the wall, some propped on top of each other, and the main street was almost too narrow for the wagon to pass. People bumped against our sides to get around us.

Of course they stared at me with mouths so wide you could see down their gullets from our higher vantage. Mothers pulled children onto their shoulders to look at me. Gasps and hollers spread through the street. Richard took no notice of this.

I should mention that both our wagons looked like typical bloated carnival wagons, with round roofs, ring-plated wheels, decorative porch guards, and faded paint over the ribs from former

attractions. On that high driver's seat I was an appropriate attraction, not some random beast. It was because of the carnival wagon that I didn't cause a panic.

"Every one of these poor sods is getting a two pence show for free," Richard said.

"Why didn't you have me go inside the wagon?"

"Because they'd throw turnips and block my path. You're my ticket back into this town. They may not know about the deal I made, but even so. A real mystical creature is in the open for them to see. I'm redeeming myself."

Once we got through the main street it forked off to less congested roads. Richard stayed on the middle path, riding past cottages and tented businesses. An area of greenery opened up with a round brick building beside it. A magistrate's sigil was on a metal post by the door.

Richard sighed and parked the wagon on the grass just off the road. "Here we go."

When I stepped down a crowd of bedraggled children caught up to us to squeal at me.

"Quite a sight, isn't he kids?" Richard said, in full carnival master character. "You tell your parents that Richard the Great has brought a real magical beast into your town. Free for all to see!"

He ignited even greater excitement in them. They couldn't stop staring at my legs and tail. I supposed I needed to get used to this.

"How can you walk on such tiny feet!" a little girl crowed.

"Just fine, and you can see."

"He talks!"

A new flurry of oos and ahhs cascaded through them.

Richard led us to the building. "Even so," he said, "it's adorable the way your little hooves click on the cobblestones."

I scoffed to try to dismiss his sweet observation.

The door swung open before Richard could knock. A stout magistrate decorated with glittering medals and with a full brown beard gaped at me.

Richard bowed in front of him. "My lord, I've brought to you a faun from the mystical realm of Schaletar. Our centerus friend could not return from his land due to his family concerns and sent this rarer creature in his stead." He rose from his bow with his charming smile in full force. "I trust this will settle our dispute."

The magistrate shoved him aside to get to me. His fat fist shot for my head and tried to pull off my horn. I shrieked.

"What are you doing!"

He released me. "It's a trick. Another con."

"I assure you it's not," Richard said, affecting a wounded voice. "For even if I could attach horns to his head there's no way I could fabricate the shape of his legs."

The magistrate gaped at them, then walked a circle around me. "It's real? A real mystical beast?"

"Of course I'm real."

He pushed against both our backs to get us in the station. The drawing room inside seemed to lead into a dwelling. I smelled the noxious fumes of meat cooking.

The magistrate went to an armchair and sat. He tented his fingers together. Richard and I stood side by side before him. (I remember this moment fondly, the solidarity between us.)

"Now then." He cleared his throat. "You've proven yourself a charlatan before, and I'm not so easily convinced. Leave the creature with me for a night and I'll run him through my own tests to make certain…" He paused, and I finally noted the lasciviousness in his eyes. "…that he's authentic."

"Anyone can see he's real just by looking at him," Richard said.

"That's exactly what a fraudster would say! Why are you afraid of scrutiny?"

Richard's face grew stern. "I'm not leaving him with anyone. He's a guest to my carnival doing a great favor to his friend."

"You're refusal just makes me certain he's another trick. Have you forgotten you're facing the hangman's noose?"

"You can make all the threats you want. I won't expose him to any unpleasantness."

His defense made me certain of his character. This wasn't false kindness. His life was at risk, and he still would not sacrifice me.

I placed a hand on Richard's shoulder. "Hold on now. I don't see how a few tests could be unpleasant." I shot the magistrate a sultry grin. "It might even be fun."

Richard's brows quivered at me. He lifted a finger at the magistrate. "Would you give us a moment to discuss this?"

He crossed his arms. "Just a moment."

We stepped outside and closed the door.

"What are you doing?" Richard whispered close to my ear.

"Getting you out of your 'pickle.'"

"That man has unsavory intentions for you."

"And you think I'm an innocent faun? I'll give him what he wants and be done with it."

Richard gasped and moved his head back to look at me. "Kali!"

I felt wounded, but persisted. "You know nothing about me, or about fauns."

"And you know nothing about perverse humans. That man might want to sodomize you."

"What is that? Sex in my ass?" I turned away. "Stop judging me and let me help you. I can give him whatever he wants and not lose a minute of sleep. The only thing that will make me feel bad is your disgusted expression."

He righted his face and swallowed. "You're right. I don't know anything about your kind—but I had respect for you."

"If you don't respect someone who will do this for you, then you never should have had any respect for me to begin with. I was a whore before you found me." I couldn't believe I said it, but once said it couldn't be taken back.

His face converted to something even worse than disgust: sympathy.

"Oh, Kali."

I would have none of it. I pushed him out of the way of the door. "Wait in the wagon." I went in and closed the door in his face.

20 Human Values

Humans are ridiculous. I presumed the magistrate wanted to fuck me, but when I stripped and posed for him, letting him 'inspect me', he did nothing but sweat and breathe heavy. After a while he said we were done and raced away to masturbate. I remained to have him assure me the troupe was pardoned. The man never touched me.

Less than an hour later I went to the wagon. Richard sat at the side table, leaning on one arm and looking miserable.

"He's convinced. The troupe is pardoned. He had a letter ready to go to the earl about your fraud and rewrote a new one about the discovery of a new kind of beast in your carnival."

Richard lifted his head. "I'm sorry you had to do that, Kali."

I got angry. "I didn't do anything. He never touched me—just looked."

He gestured for me to come to him. I entered the wagon, closed the door, and sat across from him at the table.

"I was thinking of you as a child. Something like my Maisie. That was wrong of me. You are a man. I should have had respect for you as a man."

I drew breath to speak, but he lifted a hand to quiet me.

"Look, there's no doubt you're part of our troupe now. You can't deny you're invested in staying with us after what you just did. As long as you're with me you'll never have to do anymore unsavory acts. Your past is just that, in the past.

You have a new beginning with us, and no one will know what you came from."

"I'm not some victim deserving of pity, Richard. Everything I've done in my life was what I chose to do."

"Okay. Then let me explain. Sex is a sacred act to happen only between a husband and wife. If a woman has sex outside of marriage, she's a slut who will get stoned. If a man does it he's a scoundrel. And that's not to say men don't do it, but we know it's wrong. We hide our shame."

It took a moment for this to soak in. "What of sex between a husband and husband or wife and wife?"

He became baffled. "Wife and wife? No, what you speak of is considered obscenity. A man should only be with a woman, and a woman should only be with a man." He turned away. "People who violate this are called deviants, and they're hung or burned on a pyre. That magistrate only went after you because he knew he could get away with it."

I was aghast. "This is how it is in the human world? It's insanity! How can you predict the gender of the person you'll love? Not even the centeri are so backwards. You're not a civilized people at all."

He shrugged as though he had few convictions toward the subject. "It's just how it is. I'm fascinated you see it as odd. Imagine that, a whole race of creatures who could love anyone, no matter if he was a man or woman. That's quite an intriguing concept. As for humans, our behavior reflects our religion. We've been taught very strictly what's right or wrong. Well, most people were taught, I mean. I didn't go to much church

growing up in the carnival. These rules are so ingrained in society I learned them in passing. If your values differ from ours you need to keep that to yourself. I speak with utter truth here Kali if people find out you've lain with men you'll be put to death. Mystical creature or not. You'll be cast as a demon."

I felt like weeping. "I don't want to live in this world."

He took my hand. "But it's a good world. It's a place you can recover from—"

I jerked my hand away. "I don't need to recover! Sex is lovely. It's a fine pastime. And no, I didn't care to be a whore, but it wasn't all bad. I certainly wasn't ashamed."

His eyes strayed from me. "I'd like to learn more about your world. These attitudes you have. But only confide in me, and no one else, not even Maisie. People can be petty."

"I'll do more than confide in you. I'll convince you that this cruelty you endure is uncivilized."

He grinned. "Perhaps so. But to think you have it all right and we have it all wrong is egotism. The truth probably lies somewhere in between."

That resonated, and I nodded.

Someone knocked at our door. Richard gestured with his chin for me to open it. The magistrate climbed a step to lean in.

"Are you going to be setting up in the square again?"

Richard scratched his head. "Not this time, I think. We were already done here a week ago."

"But the people will want to see your mystical creature."

"Yes, true. Though he rode on the cab all the way in. Most everyone has seen him. Have you sent that letter about him to the earl?"

"A runner is coming to fetch it."

"Well, good. Let me get the rest of my caravan and we'll discuss setting up here again."

The magistrate smiled. "Splendid. You're most welcome now." He hopped down and closed the door.

Richard scoffed. "I'll be damned if I spend another week here. They robbed us." He rose and patted my shoulder as he went by. "You stay in the wagon this time. We're getting out of here."

21 The New Actor

After Brixberry was another walled town called Claybridge. We camped on the hill overlooking it the night before heading in. Richard busied himself with working out the act for Callum and Duncan. I shifted my cushion back to the bench seat and curled my body so I could sleep there instead of the doorway. I was just settling down when Richard popped his head in calling for me.

"Kali! We need to rehearse your act."

I sat up wearily and pulled on a tunic. It was quite late.

"What act?" I said, climbing down. "I thought I was posing in the cage."

"Posing like a caged animal was good enough for the centerus. But we have an educated, well-spoken faun. I want everyone who sees you to become enchanted by your voice. I'm taking down the bars of the cage to make it a second stage."

"What do you expect me to do with only one day to prepare?"

"That poem you were reciting from before. How much do you have memorized?"

"It's a page-long poem."

Richard grew excited. "Then act it out! Spew it with all the emotion in your heart."

I put my face in my hand. "Oh, gods."

"Why gods in the plural? You saying you have more than one? Oh, never mind. After you recite the poem, you'll step down from the stage and walk through the crowds letting them all get a

good look at you. They can touch your legs for a pence."

"What happened to no unsavory acts?"

"Callum will keep guard over you." He kept smiling.

I took a deep breath. "Why are you making me do all this? Aren't I a spectacle enough as it is?"

He clutched my arm and pulled me close. "That was before we were going to have an audience with the king."

I blinked at him.

"We're going from Claybridge to Easton, the home of the earl. He'll see you're real and tell the king. Then we've got five more villages before we're at the capital. The king will want to meet you, but only if you're rumored to be a beautiful sophisticated being, not a dumb animal. Once you have an audience with the king, you'll be famous. The Grand Motley Carnival will be famous. We'll be in demand throughout the country. In other countries even!"

I groaned. "I'm not sure if I remember the verses right."

Richard's teeth sparkled. "No one will know if you say the wrong words!"

"I've never performed before."

"You'll be a natural!"

I jerked my arm away from him. "Oh stop." I went back into the wagon to practice.

***

That night Maisie quietly exited for her customary peeing. This time she was gone for more than an hour.

***

In Claybridge we set up in the town circle which had a gazebo we claimed for one of our stages. Maisie set up a violet tent covered with symbols of mysticism. Callum put on a spotted unitard that revealed the dense hair of his chest. Fergus wore a leotard with an undershirt and leggings. He practiced somersaults while I helped Richard rope off the surrounding area.

As for Duncan…he was dragging out props from the basement of the wagon while bickering with Callum. I already saw him as the sad clown Richard envisioned.

When everything was set up Richard brought us into a circle on the grass. "Right. First thing, the five pence ticket is only for the main stage. If they want to see Kali they have to pay that and another two pence. That oak will block his stage from any lookie-loos on the perimeter. Kali, sit on the edge of the stage with your legs hanging over for your performance so only the people right in front of you can see. You'll have shows at 2, 6, and 10. A half hour before noon we'll start selling tickets. At noon I'll do the intro on the gazebo stage. Fergus do your flips. Callum come on your cue and lift me up while I sit on the chair. Maisie you're still a half pence a reading. Fergus will start the show with his acrobatics. Then Callum does his strong man routine. Fergus change into the jester costume and do your juggling. I'll recite from Nye. Then we do the new act, Callum and Duncan. You need to be in full face paint by then, Duncan."

"Yeah, yeah."

"After that we'll open ticket sales for Kali. I want you at the oak making sure we don't have any sneakers, Callum."

"Oh gods," I muttered.

Richard wet his lips. "Let's run through your act now."

I nodded and rose. I went into Duncan's smaller and more crowded wagon, where I would be sequestered throughout the show. Skirting through a narrow path in the rear brought me to the hatch that led out to the cage. The bars were gone, making it a half moon stage. I clopped out with my arms hugging myself.

Richard stood in front of my stage. "No, no, don't ball up. Put your chest out. You're a magnificent beast! Show the audience how proud you are."

I grimaced at him, but then posed like a regal starlet.

"Ha ha! Wonderful, just like that!"

"Oh, shut up." I went to the edge of the stage and sat. Then I recited.

"Can't hear you! Project, project! Speak from your belly not your chest."

I still spoke from my chest, but louder. (It would take private training later for me to accomplish what Richard described.)

"Gesticulate. Open your arms. Make yourself big."

I could only do he asked by pretending to be a self-loving asshole. I was sarcastic and melodramatic.

"Right. That's good, but less obnoxious. Do it again. Be a sweet forest creature this time."

I clutched my hands together below my chin and now recited as though I were Babbette from my high school trying to woo Mr. Renherld.

"Now that was perfect! I told you you were a natural."

I sat scowling at him. He took a seat on the grass. "Now announce that you're going to give them a closer look, and that it's a pence for them to touch you."

"I'm coming down, and if you want to touch me it's a penny!"

"Not like that!"

I rolled my eyes facetiously and then assumed the persona I used as a prostitute. "Now I'll give you all a closer look. I'd be happy to let you touch my legs or tug my tail, but it will cost you a penny."

"Perfect! Beautiful! Tell Callum if they don't pay."

I put my face in my hands. My stomach was doing flips inside me.

"Kali, you'll do fine. After the three shows tomorrow you'll be able to do this in your sleep. It will grow boring and you'll ask me for a more challenging routine."

I lifted my face. "So you say."

He grinned ear to ear. "I know you won't let me down."

22 The Show

After a final run-through the next morning I was cloistered in Duncan's wagon. I sat at the miniscule half-table attached to one wall and watched the others through the window.

At 11 booming music came from the gazebo. There was a wind-up music-box with a massive cone speaker.

Something stirred within me as I heard it. This wasn't the same tune I'd listened to at carnivals I'd attended as a child, but it had the same invigorating rhythm that made you want to grab a partner and dance.

I saw people bunch around the roped-off periphery angling their heads to watch us. Richard opened the ropes to let in what looked like another magistrate and his wife and child. They carried chairs with them and set up directly before the stage. I don't believe Richard collected any money.

Duncan had set-up a dressing room on the far side of his wagon where shrubbery granted him some privacy. He appeared in garish clown make-up, with a thick red, frowning mouth and triangle eyes with tears painted down one cheek. He wore a costume I saw him sew together last night: a ragged vagrant shirt and enormous pants with suspenders.

Clowns in my world would imitate the make-up of well-to-do women, but in an exaggerated way. It astonishcd me that there were similarities to Richard's clowns. Then I thought about how we shared the word clown in common— an entire language in fact. We had to have all been one society long ago. It hurt my head to fathom it.

Duncan looked miserable and barked at the people to line up. When Richard gave him a cue he opened the rope and traded tickets for five pence pieces, which were silver and made of base metal. The spectators, likely three dozen, each brought a chair or stool, while children piled in front to sit on the grass.

Richard strode to the middle of the gazebo wearing a top hat and long velvet coat and carrying a long black cane. His face was lit up as bright as a star. His eyes gleamed and his smile looked euphoric. All chatter ceased when he appeared. I felt my heart quicken as I watched this version of Richard, who was at the peak of his glory.

"Ladies and Gentlemen, lovely children from two to teen, welcome to the new Grand Motley Carnival!"

His voice carried through the audience with contagious exuberance. The people applauded energetically until he continued.

"I look upon you beautiful people, you good farmers, wives, maids and merchants. I see a crowd of ordinary folk about to become extraordinary—for today my wonderful crowd you shall see sights that will crumble the walls of your great town! Everything you think impossible shall be possible this day, and so the world shall open to untold possibility!" He leaned down to address a boy seated in front. "Do you think me a liar?" He pointed his cane at a grandmother in the seats. "Do you doubt my words could be true?"

"No!" came the shouts in return.

"My good people, the earl and our own noble king wait to see the wonder you shall be the first to witness this day. In that wagon, yes, the very one behind you, is not a man, not a centerus,

but a creature so new and so real your minds shall explode at the wonder of him. A faun my dear ladies and gentleman! From beyond the cliffs of death, in the faraway land of Schaletar, I have brought a half-man half-sheep! Yes, you heard right! Yes, he is real! So real you can tug his tail and pull on his horns!"

They better not.

The crowd ooed and ahhed, craning their heads back towards the wagon I was in. One man pointed at me in the window. I pulled the curtain in front of me closed. This was caught by nearly all the audience and ignited a fervor through them. Now people were standing and chattering rapidly to each other about the white-haired man with horns.

"Now, now, good people." Their focus returned to Richard. "I understand your excitement. Why my heart practically burst from my chest when I saw the beautiful, mystical Kali!"

Beautiful? My cheeks got warm.

"But he is for later, my dear folks."

They gave sounds of disappointment and a few boos.

"For now…"

On this cue Fergus did back flips across the stage. The crowd was won again. They cheered and hooted. A soon as Fergus passed, Callum entered. He went to the edge of the stage, spread his massive arms, and growled at the children. They screamed and laughed. Callum put a chair in the middle of the stage and Richard sat in it, holding the edges beside his hips.

"We have acrobats, we have jugglers, we have mystics who can tell you your future! And now dear people…"

Callum gripped a leg of the chair and lifted Richard over his head with one hand.

"I present Callum! Strongest man in the world!"

The crowd cheered and clapped, a few people even standing.

Callum set him down and left the stage. Fergus flip-flopped back in keeping everyone's attention through Richard's last announcements.

"Your ticket today has bought you the magnificent show on this stage! At two, remain in the ropes and go to the wagon stage. You'll spend but two pennies more to see the gorgeous, magical creature Kali."

Gorgeous now? I enjoyed his hyperbole.

They shrieked with excitement.

"But wait! The magic and amazement doesn't end there." He pointed to Maisie's purple tent. "We have with us the greatest mystic in the world. Blessed by the holy God of man, she has the gift of sight into your future. She can tell you the name of the man you'll marry, the names of the children you'll have, and can warn you of any coming misfortune! Own your fate rather than be owned by it. For a mere half-penny, get a reading with the Lady Amalthia!"

More applause followed. My word, he could sell. The people were bubbling with excitement in their seats. Even I felt infected by it. For a moment I believed there was a true fortune-teller in that tent, and not Richard's annoying wife.

"Now, without further pause, let the show begin!"

He vacated the stage and Fergus took over. He spread his body on a giant hoop to spin and flip for them. Everything he did, even his meager hand-

walking, harvested cheers from the giddy crowd. He closed by climbing onto the fence of the gazebo and performing flips on its hexagonal fence. I was thoroughly impressed.

After he took his bows Callum got on the stage and antagonized the audience as part of his routine. Good-natured heckling came back to him. He called up the children to climb onto a bench, lifted them high, and spun them while they screamed with glee.

The door burst open and Fergus ran in. He grinned at me, but then hastily stripped and got into a one-piece jester costume with ostrich feather wig. As Callum finished his show of strength by bending a skillet, Fergus painted a black mask around his eyes at the shard of mirror nailed to the post of a bunk bed. He looked like a completely different performer than he had as an acrobat. He opened a trunk and took out a burlap bag filled with balls and batons then zipped away.

He got on stage after Callum left, performing an amazing juggling act. I grew sick. I had zero talent and yet I was a fellow actor to a man who could do standing back flips and juggle fire-lit torches. What right had I to be there?

Then I remembered. I was a mystical faun.

Duncan came in and used the same mirror as Fergus to touch up his clown make-up.

"Dumbest fucking shit I ever done in my life," he said to his reflection.

"I think you look amazing."

Now he scowled at me. "I'm a fucking clown. My whole life I said I'd never be a clown and now look at me!"

I shook my head, confused. "What's wrong with being a clown?"

He scoffed. "You'll see."

With that he exited.

Fergus took another bow before the standing ovation he received, and then Richard entered the stage. His long coat was replaced by a hooded cloak. He stood in the middle of the stage until the crowd became silent, then drew back the hood.

"To live, or not to live. This is the infernal question which troubles the minds of men..."

I pulled back the curtain in full, no longer caring if someone glimpsed me. Not that anyone would. All were mesmerized by Richard, myself included. His words put a quiver in my belly, it made my heart thud. It was as if he cast a spell using his luscious face, his scintillating voice, and the slow methodical movements he highlighted his speech with.

I tell you, it was truly an amazing thing I beheld. We had an acrobat, a man of incredible strength, and then a riveting juggler. You would think a man orating could not compete, but he actually surpassed them. The audience was entranced with agape mouths. When he came to a sad passage, I saw wives cling to their husband's in tears. The adventure part had them sit up in their seats as though running with the bandit he described. We saw not Richard, but the thrilling parable his words painted. And then, the end, the happy ending. I couldn't help but cheer with the rest of the crowd. I was tearful, elated—totally removed from that wagon where I watched.

I could not believe how magnificent Richard was.

He escaped the stage after three bows to the roars of the crowd. They still clapped for him when

he circled behind the bushes to get to the wagon. He burst in.

"Okay Kali, we're going to…" His lips parted. "What's wrong?"

My eyes were puffy with tears. "Nothing."

He knelt down and took both my hands in his. "Don't be scared, Kali. You're going to be wonderful."

"It's not that," I said, wiping a tear. "It was your oration."

A smile slowly lit up on his face. "Really?"

I couldn't hold back the emotion in my voice. "It was so beautiful."

He laughed, also getting emotional. "Thank you. If you appreciate it then I know I'm still doing something right." He stood. "But as nice as that is, get yourself together."

He went to a cupboard and poured me some water in a chipped mug. I took it with both hands and sipped.

"I want you to sit at this window and watch Duncan collecting the fee for you. Don't come out until all the people are past him, and even then wait a few moments for them to settle in. When you come out hold your head high and stand still at the center of the stage for them to absorb their first look at you. When their amazement dies down begin your speech. Say it as you go to the edge of the stage and sit down."

I swallowed and nodded my head.

Then Richard cradled the side of my face with his hand. "And you're going to do great. Believe in yourself because I believe in you."

I managed a smile, and he left the wagon.

The tender touch seemed natural when it happened. Afterwards, with the echo of his fingers

against my cheek, I realized the intimacy his caress conveyed. Would he ever touch Duncan or Callum in that way? No. Maisie perhaps, but not another man. I wondered if Richard still did not see me as a man, but as some gentler creature closer to a woman. I could not decide how I felt about that.

This wasn't the time to ponder. I missed Callum and Duncan's act, though I do recall they got shrieks of laughter. Richard was on the stage now.

"Did you enjoy the show my good people?"

The responded with cheers.

"Would you like to see the faun now?"

Even greater cheers erupted.

"Stay within the ropes, for once you leave it's five pence to get back in. But since you've already paid those five pence, you have only to pay two pence more for Kali's show. Please head back where our clown Duncan is waiting at the stage connected to the wagon. And tell your friends and neighbors to attend our magnificent carnival. We have three shows a day, at noon, four, and eight."

Every person in attendance bought entry to my show. I watched Duncan collecting their money with my heart racing. They crowded in the smaller area before my stage. When the last one went through I rose to my shaking legs and braced myself with my hand on my heart.

With a final deep breath, I exited the hatch. The back of the stage was in deep shadow, but I already caused hurried talk and gasps. I stepped to the sunlight in the middle and froze while looking upwards. Now the hurried talk exploded into a roar of sound.

"It's a beast! A real beast!"

"How could they fake those legs? It's a real thing I tell you!"

"Watch how it walks. That will tell us if it's a trick."

"But it's got the horns of a ram and the legs of one too."

"I've got to get my mother here. She needs to see this before she dies."

This went on for minutes. I waited, stricken in my pose but hoping it didn't show. As long as I kept my eyes off the crowd I could hold my composure.

"Is the night not a spear…"

The start of my oration riled them up all over again.

"It can talk, it can talk!"

"It spoke, did you hear it?"

This time I waited only a few moments before continuing. It wasn't until the third verse that they settled down and actually listened. I finally looked at them, a good forty people and half again in children. There wasn't space for their chairs so they stood in a clump to watch me. I kept reciting, not missing a word, and not letting a quaver infect my frightened voice. I tried to imitate the majesty I'd seen in Richard.

He stood at the side of the crowd with Callum, watching me with an expression of ardor. His head was cocked and his eyes glassy. I focused on him for a few choice lines.

"But when one can love, they find it anywhere. Love's lure can't be restrained."

I don't know what my intention was, but if asked I could say I was simply reciting.

I gave the last line and then bowed my head.

They didn't erupt in cheers, but clapped. The conversation started again with everyone trying to figure me out.

"Now my good people, I know it's hard to believe I'm truly a faun. I would like to walk among you so you can see me up close. If you wish to touch me, you must pay a pence for the privilege."

"Make way, make way!" Callum said, addressing the front of the crowd.

They opened a space for me to descend into them. Amazed men and women now stood mere feet from me. They opened a path as I moved through them.

"But what are you?" a woman said.

"I'm a faun."

Her question opened the floodgates for more. They said too many at once and then one person managed to be heard.

"How did you get here?"

I addressed the man who asked. "I came through a passage in the mountains."

"What other creatures are on the other side of the death cliffs?"

I paused, because I only knew of centeri and fauns. Richard's speech at the beginning made me think I should not limit their imagination.

"There are centeri and fauns and a great many other races. I swore to my…er…king that I wouldn't let the humans know about any race they haven't already encountered."

"But why not? Why not?"

"I think he's afraid. He wouldn't wish for any of our peoples to be hunted."

"But are there mermaids?"

I grinned mischievously. "Don't tell my king I told you, but yes, there are mermaids."

They looked at each other in gleeful awe.

The magistrate who'd gotten in for free pushed his way through the crowd to get to me. "All right, look here. This is all too strange if you ask me. You said it's a pence to touch you, well here." He took a coin out of his pocket and held it out for me. It was larger than a pence or a five pence and silver in color. "Here's a quarter if I can give a good pull on your horns."

I balked. "But you'll hurt me."

He snuffled. "If I'm hurting you I'll stop, but if they're fake they're coming off."

I peeked at Richard through the crowd.

"You don't have to, Kali," he said with a stern face, putting my wellbeing over money, as always.

I took the coin from him. "Okay."

He grabbed both my horns and tried to pull them apart. I cried out in pain. He let go suddenly.

"God, I'm sorry! I thought they were fake!"

I didn't understand his reaction until I felt the trickle of blood on my forehead. Both roots of my horns throbbed.

I wiped it away with a pitiful expression. "It's all right."

"Oh, the poor thing."

"So he's real! He's really real!"

A few more pennies were offered to touch my tail and hooves. Callum started calling for the crowd to go once it was clear no one else was willing to pay. Richard collected me and put me back into the wagon. He found a rag and soaked it to wipe the blood from my hair.

"That ass! We're not going to let anyone else abuse you. If they ask you say it's not allowed. I'll have Callum back you if there's trouble."

"It's fine. It didn't hurt that much."

He remained firm. "It's not fine for someone to make you bleed."

"Do you want the quarter, Richard?"

"The what? No, no, no. That's your money."

"So this is my pay? What I make at the end of my recitals?"

Richard grimaced and moved to sit at the other chair of the table. "No. That's not usually how we do it. I suppose we should have a talk about that." He felt inside his cheek with his tongue a moment. "What do you think would be fair?"

"Richard, I have no idea how much your money is worth. We don't have quarters in my land."

"A quarter is twenty-five pence." He folded his hands on the narrow table. "You have a farthing, which is a quarter pence, a half-pence, a pence, a five pence, a ten pence, a quarter, and a pound. A pound is one hundred pence."

"But what is the real value? What can a quarter buy me?"

"A quarter is quite a sum, actually. A quarter could get you a night at one of the royal inns in the capital."

"That doesn't tell me much. Put it in terms of food."

"For twenty-five pence you could buy half the carcass of a sheep."

I cringed. They ate sheep here? Certain aspects of the human world were truly disgusting.

"In terms of food I actually eat."

"Oh right. I'd say you could get ten bushels of wheat and another two bushels of apples."

This struck me. "Oh," I said with a nod.

"For this show we made two pounds and forty pence. That's eighty pence more than usual because of your show. If you were Duncan, Callum, or Fergus you'd expect your share to be half of what your act made. But you're new. If I give you that much the others might get mad."

"How much are the three of them each getting from this show?"

"It works out like this. Maisie gets half of whatever she brings in from her tent and the rest is put into the pot. Her pay is really just some spending money since I provide for her. We've got two more shows today and I'm hoping this will be the worst of them. But if this was all we made in a day, and if you weren't here, half the pot would go to me and the remainder would be split evenly between Duncan, Callum, and Fergus. So one pound twenty for me and forty pence each for them."

My brow strained in thought. "You made eighty pence from my first show."

"Correct."

"So had I not been here you would have made..." I calculated on the concave ceiling. "One pound and sixty pence. Half of that is...eighty pence. If you split that into three that's about 25 pence for each of them."

"Right, right. So if you weren't here, their shares would probably be 26 pence. Let's say we give you an equal share with them. They're splitting one pound twenty into four ways. That's thirty pence for each."

"And more than they would make if I weren't here, even though it's four shares now instead of three."

He nodded resolutely. "They can't complain about that."

"You can add the money I make from the groping to the pot."

He fumed in consideration. "You made thirty pence today just from that. You're the biggest money-maker for me in the carnival right now. That should earn you a premium."

I squeezed his hand. "You're very fair, Richard. I like that about you." I removed my hand. "Still, all I did is say a poem and let people touch me. Fergus works the hardest. He should get the largest share."

"Fergus' father does the least and gets the same share as him. When he was my centerus, which I didn't charge a separate fee for because I didn't want the scrutiny, he was a big draw for the carnival. Now he's doing work I could pay any farm boy fifty pence a week for. I'm giving Duncan a share for Fergus' sake. That's the only reason."

I put the quarter in his hand. "Give me half the groping money and put the other half in the workers' share."

He thought it over and then nodded. "Okay. That's acceptable. You're going to need to keep track because if Callum collects the money it's going right into the pot."

He scraped the legs of the chair on the floor to stand. "I need to get things ready for the next show. There's no food left for a lunch, but I'll send Maisie out later to fetch victuals for a big dinner."

"You provide our food?"

"I provide the wagons, the equipment, and all the communal meals. That's why I get the lion's share."

I stood before he left. "Richard. I have one more question. How much would another wagon cost?"

"A wagon and another set of horses, you mean?"

I nodded.

"Two hundred to three hundred pounds, depending on how close we are to the capital."

I smiled. "Thank you."

23 Money

The second performance was easier for me. I understood my audience now and found them less intimidating. This crowd was larger than the first, but the last had a crowd of more than a hundred adults, mostly men.

After the final show I was released from my prison in the wagon and sat with the others around the fire. Maisie had brought meat on skewers, garlic bread, roasted potatoes, and hunks of cheese. The last item was for me, but I wouldn't eat it. Cheese was made from the milk of cows. If I won't eat the flesh of a cow why would I eat its issuance? I was happy enough with the delicious bread and potatoes.

When we'd all quenched our hunger Richard took out a velvet sack with a gold ribbon pull string. It was bulging with coins.

"All right my friends, as you know we had a terrific day."

Callum and Maisie gave hurrahs while Fergus clapped.

"The final take for the night, deducting nothing for this feast, is 12 pounds and fifty pence."

The hurrahs were louder now.

Duncan looked up, flabbergasted. "That's almost as much as we made a day in the capital."

"That's thanks to Kali's show. Almost four pounds came just from him."

"That's one way to put it," Callum said, flaring his nostrils with a snuffle. "See, if you made any of us do one of these little add-on shows we could have brought in that money just the same. He

didn't do anything great for us. It's just the way you structured it. You could have put the oration, juggling, and acrobat on the main stage and then charge two pence more if they wanted to see the strong man."

"No one's paying two pence extra to see your act," Duncan said.

"Oh? What's your act again? Nothing. That's right."

"My act used to be letting people see a real life centerus. The question I have is why weren't you charging two pence extra for people to see me?"

"Because you weren't real," Richard said. "It's bad enough we were trying to get away with a fraud. If we added insult by making a premium from it we would have just been caught sooner."

"Maybe we would have, maybe we wouldn't have," Duncan said.

Fergus used his hands to say something lengthy.

"Shut up you ass," Callum said to him. (I hadn't realized he knew the symbol language as well.)

"What did he say?" I asked Richard.

"Yeah," Maisie said.

"He said the only act we had that might have been worth an extra two pence before Kali was his juggling, but if we took that out of the main act we would have gone below two hours and people would have called it a rip-off."

"Your juggling ain't so great," Callum said.

"Yes it is," I said. Fergus smiled at me.

"Shut your mouth. You just fucking got here. What makes you think you got a say in anything?"

"I saved your lives."

Callum's mouth twitched as though trying to find something to say.

"Well said, Kali," Richard said. "Now it's my turn to state some facts. There was no draw in our carnival that was worth a two pence add-on before Kali came. I never even considered that structure because it would have given us unhappy crowds and a reputation as rip-offs. We charged two pence extra for them to see our real faun. Not one person complained. Not one person left here unsatisfied. They were happy to pay that premium because Kali is truly that amazing."

Duncan and Callum scoffed.

"I'm not taking anything away from the rest of you. Duncan, you did fine as a clown today."

"Oh, please."

"And Callum you're not just two out of five of my main stage acts, you're the man I rely on to protect the rest of us."

He flared his nostrils again.

"Fergus, I'm sure I need not tell you how outstanding you are. I'd be lucky to find even one of your talents in another man, let alone two."

He nodded.

"That said, the five of us are a five pence show. That's the reality. If I could have charged more, I would have. The only reason we made an extra four pounds today is because we have a real faun, the only one on this side of the world, the only real mystical creature these people will ever see in their lives."

"All right enough of this horse-shit," Callum said. "What's the break down?"

Richard turned up a hand. "Kali gets an equal share."

Neither Callum nor Duncan replied.

"And his groping money is going in the pot. Is that clear then? We all understand?"

"So give us our fucking money."

Richard tossed the bag in front of Maisie. "It's one pound fifty-six pence for each of you. Maisie will count it out."

24 Betrayal

That night Maisie once again left to pee and didn't return in the short time it should have taken her. I woke up halfway when the door clicked, but then fell back into a dead sleep. I woke up fully when Richard pulled the chair on the other side of my bench bed to sit down. I used the table to pull myself up.

"It's the second night she's done this."

I blinked at him. "Go out and look for her."

He let out a sigh that quavered with agony. I made myself sit fully upright.

"Go out and look and find her with my acrobatic juggler, or my strong man, or Duncan." He tipped up his nose. "If it was Duncan, I'd throw him out. It would be nice to get rid of him. But I doubt it's him. He's too old for her." His head slowly shook. "I can't afford to lose Callum or Fergus."

"Is this the first time she's done something like this?"

His brow rose. "The first time? No. We went back for a show in her home town. She made time with a boy she'd grown up with. I found her sitting on his lap at the inn and told her she could stay with him." He lifted his head to meet my eyes. "I guess he didn't want her. She came running back begging for forgiveness. At the time I didn't think they'd slept together. I forgave her." His chest rose and fell with a sigh. "Things were good between us after that." He rose a finger with a thought. "You know, I thought things were good between us lately, too." His hand lowered. "I was obviously wrong."

"She's making a mistake. You're a good man."

He interlaced his fingers. "Yes. I thought I was too." He grimaced. "I'm sorry I shouldn't be keeping you up."

"It's all right, Richard. We're friends."

He smiled. "You know, I don't think I've had a friend in this troupe before. I like Fergus very much, but he'll always side with his father. I can only get so far with him." He tore a bit of dry skin from his lip. "Why do you think she's unhappy with me?"

"I can't answer that."

"No?"

"I think you can, though."

"Hm." He focused on the table. "She's always wanted a baby. When we first married I wouldn't touch her because she was so young. Now we've been trying, oh, for two years. Nothing seems to be happening."

"So she thinks you can't get her pregnant, and she's trying to get it done with someone else?"

He put his forehead in his hands. "Oh God, now that you've said it, it seems obvious. That's just how her mind works."

I felt repulsed. "Richard, do you love her?"

"I thought I did."

"Do you love her enough to let her cheat on you and rear another man's child?"

He shook his head without looking up.

"Then maybe...I mean, you should divorce her."

He peeked up. "Really? Does it have to go all the way to that? Just because she's stupid?"

"If you let her do this to you, then she's not the only one who's stupid."

He laughed. "Right." He dragged himself to his feet. "Of course. Thank you, Kali. That's what I needed to hear."

I shrugged.

He went back into his bed and a minute later Maisie joined him.

She smelled like sex. If I could smell it I was certain Richard could as well.

25 Revelations

I should note that though my time with access to a bathtub was over, we still washed. Richard was fastidious about it, cleaning with a basin behind his curtain every other day. Callum or I would go to brooks we passed to fill buckets with water that would be poured into barrels inside each of the wagons. We were by no means filthy.

***

On the second day of the show Fergus burst into the wagon to change into his jester costume.

I tried to hold my tongue. I really couldn't. Richard had made me care about him.

"Fergus?"

He glanced at my reflection in his chunk of mirror.

"You're not sleeping with Maisie, are you?"

He faced me and shook his head broadly from side to side. Then he lifted one hand to indicate someone very tall.

"It's Callum?"

He nodded with wide eyes. Then he turned back to the mirror to finish drawing his mask.

I was glad it wasn't Fergus because I liked him. Callum and Maisie were two I already disliked. They deserved each other.

Richard came into the wagon after Fergus left. He went to the bunk bed, pulled off the blanket of the top mattress, and sniffed it.

"It's Callum, Richard."

His eyes darted to me.

"Fergus just told me."

"Damn it." He turned his back and clenched a fist. I could see his arm shaking. "Damn, damn, damn it." He ripped open the door and stormed out.

After Callum and Duncan's act he went on the gazebo to close the main show. His character was perfect. His voice still fostered excitement. The only hint of his anger was how brusquely he stomped off the stage.

I didn't see him in the audience of my show later, just the repulsive Callum.

At dinner that night he was still missing.

"Where the fuck is Richard?" Callum said.

"Oh, he'll pay us tomorrow night," Duncan said. "You know he's always good about that."

"Yeah, well he better."

Maisie moved from near me to sit beside Callum. The two whispered. I exchanged a look with Fergus who flashed an expression of dread.

An hour after we bedded down Richard entered and settled in with Maisie. Even though I was further from them on the table bench bed, I could still hear every soft word they said.

"Where were you?" Maisie said.

"No where in particular."

"The men were angry they didn't get paid."

"I'll settle with them tomorrow."

"That was rude of you, Richard."

"I suppose it was. Speaking of rude, where have been going the last two nights when you disappear for an hour at a time?"

"To get fresh air. To walk, to think. I'm not a prisoner am I?"

"Do you swear that's all you've been doing? Will you look me in my eye and swear it?"

"What's wrong with you! You're being such an ass tonight."

"That's what I thought."

"What do you mean that's what you thought? Don't turn away from me."

"Goodnight, Maisie."

It got quiet for a moment.

"You're going to lose everything if you don't wise up, Richard."

"I know."

Then they both stayed silent. Maisie didn't leave the wagon that night.

26 The Posters

After three days of shows I helped the others put an entire carnival back into the crates of two wagons. I wouldn't have thought it possible, but everything was folded, collapsed, and scrunched away in its assigned space.

I joined Richard on the driver's seat again because there was no traffic on the dirt and packed grass roads we took. It seemed as though every human was walled inside their towns, never leaving. I would have loved to ask about this and a few other things that addled me, but I could see Richard needed to be alone with his thoughts.

He spoke after a day and a half of quiet travel when the next town appeared far before us. This was a massive city with walls that curved over pasture and hillside. In the center I saw the parapets of a castle.

"This is Easton, the home of Earl Chantwell. He'll have gotten that magistrate's letter by now. I'm going to go to the castle to see if he'll give you an appointment."

I blinked at him. "An appointment for what?"

"To meet you. To see with his own eyes you're real. It's a courtesy. You're something magnificent and unbelievable. I'm bringing you into Chantwell's city. He should get a private viewing of the faun show."

I shrugged. "Okay. That sounds fine."

"We should try to get the earl to sponsor the carnival. Be sure to tell him how we lost all our money in Brixberry and are struggling. Tell him we're in desperate need of a third wagon." He

glanced at me. "That is, if he takes a shine to you, of course. If he isn't interested, then leave him be."

"What do we have to give him in return for his sponsorship?"

"I don't know. Probably nothing except special treatment every time we visit his city. If he gives us a wagon, we'll paint his seal on the side of it." He pulled back on the reins to make the horses stop. "We're close enough. Get inside the wagon."

There was an expansive park in Easton where other vendors had set up camp. We claimed a spot over a cobblestone labyrinth and began to set up. Since there were so many people around I had to remain sequestered in the wagon.

Richard came in at dusk with his hair mussed from a fast ride on one of our horses. He joined me at the table. "The earl is going to send someone to have a look at you during our show to determine that you're real. Then we'll get an appointment with him."

I spread my lips in a smile. "Wonderful."

He fixed on the wall with his eyes glimmering. "Yes. But I'll go with you. The chance to connect with an earl is gigantic. We'll make good use of it."

Since there was no gazebo, a stage was built by bunching the crates together and pinning a blanket over them. They'd used this set-up frequently and produced a level stage that looked as though it had been built for them.

I saw a man in a garish scarf ride up on a horse covered in drapery with a royal seal. He dismounted and went to Richard, who was close to our wagon.

"Ah," Richard said, greeting him with a bow. "You must be the earl's man to check on our faun."

"No, good sir." The man spoke through his upward pointing nose. "I am the royal portrait maker. I've gotten word of your mystical beast and now that I'm here I see you have no posters, no banners, no sign such a creature is carried by you, nor anything to announce any of the shows you put on."

Richard's smile lost its sincerity. "We've had a bit of a rough patch."

"And it will likely remain so, unless you allow me to create banners worthy of your great show." He pulled a thick diary sized book of canvases of out of his pocket. "Here are my cameos."

Richard flipped through it stone-faced. They could have been masterpieces or rubbish. His expression indicated neither.

"How much do you propose to charge for these banners?"

"Why, I can wall one side of a wagon with a rubber-backed cloth banner seven feet high and four feet wide, perfectly lettered to your orders, for only fifteen pounds."

Richard handed him back his book. "I'm not sure if you heard me when I said we're going through a rough patch."

"I heard," the weaslely man said undaunted. "But here you are in the great city of Easton. You'll surely make a purse more than sufficient to pay me."

"At fifteen pounds I would have to rob my workers for your fee."

"Your workers shall be immortalized on canvas. Here." He offered his book again. "Show them my skill and they'll contribute towards their banners."

Richard took the book and put it in his pocket. "I would have posters of five feet high and half that wide, and I would pay three pounds a piece for them."

"Oh but—"

"I normally pay two pounds fifty to Lamont Redd. I'm sure you've heard of him."

The artist pursed his lips.

"If you can't take three pounds each for the banners, I'll hold off until I see Lamont next spring."

He looked Richard over. "And how many banners would you purchase?"

"One for myself, one for my strong man, one to be shared between my juggler and acrobat, and one for my faun."

I noticed he didn't mention a banner for Maisie.

The artist's lips twisted toward his thin mustache. "I shall give you four banners, on rubber and cloth, five feet high and two-and-a-half feet wide, for twenty pounds." He shoved out his hand to close the deal.

"Absolutely not."

"Fifteen then! And you'll let me keep a cameo of your faun." His hand jutted higher.

Richard turned his head away. "That might be reasonable, but I'll have to consult my crew. Come back tomorrow for your answer."

The artist took a deep bow. "I shall, and I shall entrust my book of cameos to you until then." He got back on his horse and left.

Richard backed to our wagon and handed me the cameo book through the window. I eagerly flipped through the portraits. They were drawn with immense skill.

"What do you say, Kali? Will you contribute one pound seventy-five of your pay for a banner?"

"If my math is correct, each banner will cost you close to four dollars. You're going to pay the greater share?"

"No, we each pay half. I'll offer him three pounds fifty for each banner and he'll accept, because he's no royal artist. He's a street vendor. He painted the earl's seal on his horse's cover to try to con us."

"His work is superb, all the same."

"Yes. He'll do a lovely portrait of you."

"Of course I'll contribute." I handed him back the book.

"Perfect. Now I've got to appeal to the vanity of Callum and Fergus."

This is how my poster came to be. On top were the words: 'Mystical Faun.' Below that it said: 'Half Man, Half Sheep.' Along the side of my crouching naked body it read: 'Touch him! Pull his tail! Tug his horns! This mystical beast IS REAL!' It was sealed to the door of the wagon so the back window would remain uncovered.

Richard's poster's was affixed to the opposite side of our wagon. It was a painting of him in his cloak with his eyes obscured in shadow and his hands gesturing outward in stark perspective. 'Richard the Magnificent' was the logo on top. 'Orator of the Greatest Works to Man! Spellbinder of Audiences Great and Wide!'

Callum's banner had him holding up one of the wagons. 'Callum the Great! Strongest Man in the World!' In diffidence to Duncan half his clown body peeked into the scene behind Callum. (This infuriated him.)

Fergus was represented as twins, one juggling fire sticks and the other upside-down in a flip. 'World's Greatest Juggler! World's Greatest Acrobat!'

On the third night of our shows in Easton I came into the wagon and heard Maisie sobbing behind her curtain. I ignored her, but Richard could not.

"What is it?"

"Why don't I have a banner?"

"You don't need one. Your tent attracts the crowds."

"But what about when we're driving through the towns?"

"Where would I put another poster? There's no room."

"There's room on the back! You're just being cross with me! Always so cross!"

"I don't want to talk about this."

"You're a vicious, vicious man!"

"Then why don't you go sleep with Callum?"

"What are you talking about?"

"Just shut up then."

She sobbed a while, and then said, "I hate you."

Richard didn't answer.

27 The Earl

The crowds in Easton were better dressed, freer with their coins, and more numerous than in Claybridge. They were less gregarious with their cheers and applause, but still beamed with excited faces. When I walked among them after my recitals, dozens upon dozens would pay to touch me. Some would even pay without touching me, as though so entranced they felt the need to give me a tip. When their hands came upon me they stroked my arms or shins like one would pet a cat.

I marked Easton in my mind as a place I would be happy to live in if I one day ended my tour with the carnival. It smelled nice here due to gutters that carried effluence to underground sewers. I saw great wealth and little poverty.

From our camp we could view a brick bakery that sold a fluffy almond cookie and nothing else. Richard told me that was the sign of a rich city when a business so specialized could still prosper. It meant the people had so much money they sought novelty rather than sustenance.

On the fourth day and final show of our successful run in Easton a man remained in the audience outside my stage. Callum tried to usher him away in the gentler manner he assumed around rich people.

"I have been sent by the earl to make sure the faun is genuine. Your carnival master is expecting me."

Callum sought Richard who brought the man to me inside Duncan's wagon.

He was in his forties and smooth-faced with parted brown hair. "Are you truly a half sheep from the land of Schaletar? If you lie you shall be put to death."

"In my land I'm not half of anything, just a faun. I'm exactly what I appear to be. It would be impossible to bend my legs this way if I were a human in a costume."

The man reached down to feel the tendon of my ankle. He shook his head with astonishment.

"How can this be?"

"He came from the other side of the death cliffs," Richard said.

"That's impossible."

"No, my lord. I found a passage and went through the rocks."

"Will other creatures follow you? Will armies?"

I was perplexed. "I doubt that. None of my kind lives anywhere near these mountains. The passage was extremely hard to find."

"But what is your purpose in this land? Explain that to me."

I exchanged a look with Richard. "I came to join this carnival. I have no prospects at home."

He broke into a smile. "Is that all? You were a pauper seeking prosperity?"

"Not a pauper, exactly. I'd been robbed. I didn't have any family or friends to help me."

The man clasped my hands. "Oh, it's all well. You seem perfectly harmless. And of course we're delighted to have one of your kind in our land. One, mind you. Not a hundred or a thousand."

I tried to smile through my confusion.

He stood and looked at Richard. "Oh yes, you're very welcome to have an audience with the

earl. I shall arrange it and fetch you tomorrow when he's ready."

Richard's eyes brightened. "Tomorrow? That's wonderful. We'll stay right here and wait for you."

We did more than wait because the carnival had to be torn down. I put on Richard's black cloak so I could go outside to help. The onlookers didn't take note of me.

Before we were done, the smooth-faced man returned this time in the cab of a regal pink carriage. He beckoned for Richard to come to him. I went too, lowering my hood to show him I was the faun.

We sat side by side and he sat across from us.

"Oh Chantwell is beside himself with excitement to meet you. He still doesn't entirely believe it's true. It's hard to convince people of such a fantastic occurrence."

"It is fantastic," Richard said. "That's why we knew we had to extend this courtesy to his grace."

I became entranced by the sights outside the carriage window. We were headed to the large castle at the center of the city. How exciting my life had become. I truly felt like a celebrity.

The carriage stopped in a round castle driveway in front of massive steps flanked by statues. We exited, and the driver continued off (to a stable, I presume). The stairs led into a gargantuan foyer with a ceiling so high I got dizzy when I craned back my head. The man led us through the tiled area and up another set of short stairs leading to a space with fountains, tapestries, and gargantuan bronze vases. To the side of this room was another set of stairs, this time carpeted.

We entered a corridor lined with doors with an atrium at the end filled with plants and numerous cushioned chairs.

This was where we met the earl, a man of fifty with ashen skin and deep sunken eyes. His body was thin except for his bulbous lower belly. Beside him was a maid holding a tray of fruit and another women spread on a chaise lounge dressed as a noble. The earl sat up when I appeared.

"There it is, Wanda."

The woman sat up as well and gasped.

Richard pulled his cloak off me so they could further show their astonishment at my legs. Then the earl's head cocked and his hands clasped together.

"Oh, why he's beautiful. Come here, come here. Sit with us."

I sat in the chair in front of him while Richard took a seat on a couch a short distance away.

"My word…can I touch your legs?"

I extended one for his pleasure.

"Oh, you must tell me all about you. Magnificent thing!"

I did with little trouble. The earl did not seem like royalty to me, but a kindly stranger. I told him about Schaletar and how civilized our society was. I told him about my work in Calico (without divulging the nature) and how I was robbed and wandered into Richard's carnival.

The earl placed a hand on my leg and left it there as he spoke.

"Oh, we are so honored to have you. You beautiful creature! You must thing I'm foolish to gush over you so."

"Not at all. I think I've gotten used to it."

"I would have you at my party tonight. Do you think you could attend?"

"Of course, if it would please you."

"My guests will be so delighted to meet you. So amazed."

"Could Richard join me?"

"Sure, sure." He acknowledged him. "You're Richard, the carnival master? Pleased to meet you."

They shook hands.

Then the earl leaned in close with both his hands propped on my naked thighs. "Now Kali, our parties get very raucous. You're not a prudish little thing, are you?"

"I'm not. I think humans are the prudish ones."

The earl and the woman laughed.

"Yes a lot of the villagers are. But we like to have fun. Do you like to have fun, Kali?"

"Yes."

"Do you know the type of fun I speak of?"

"Sex?"

The woman and he erupted in laughter again. I tried to ignore how Richard's eyes seared into me.

"Oh my word. Tell me how much fun you fauns like to have?"

"We spread our love freely, without restriction, to any and all who'd please us."

The earl grew amazed. "Why you're more magnificent all the time!" He looked at Richard. "My word, you must tell me how much to buy him."

Richard balked. "He's not my property."

"Of course I'm joking." He stated this without humor, then fixed on me once more. "Kali, darling, could you have fun with this sweet old

earl?" He brushed some hair off my cheek. "A royal shouldn't demean himself with begging, but oh, I'm begging for you my sweet thing."

I glanced at the woman and saw glittering eyes and an expectant smile.

"I wouldn't protest."

"Wouldn't you now?"

"But it's only that Richard will think very little of me if I give my favors so freely."

He scowled. "Richard? Who's Richard?" He noticed him again. "Oh. Are you a prude my good sir?"

Richard forced a smile. "I suppose I'm a typical villager."

"How wretched." He combed his fingers through the hair at my temples, beneath my horns. "A kiss then. Give me a kiss you beautiful thing."

I wrapped my arms around him and joined our mouths. Richard had to be watching, and yet I didn't hold back. I merged our tongues while caressing his back. When I released him he flopped back in his long chair as though I'd drained his life.

"Oh…I'm defeated. Destroyed!" He draped an arm across his eyes. "Never have I been so smitten!"

"May I kiss him also?" said the woman.

He righted himself. "No you harlot, he's mine!" They both erupted into more laughter. "Well I still insist you come to my party. Even if I must suffer your chaperone." He clapped and a male servant appeared. "Giles, take these two to a guest room and find them some appropriate attire for our soiree tonight."

We followed the servant to a vacant bedroom and then were left alone. (The room was lavish, with a canopied bed and ornate dark wood

furniture.) I sat on the bed while Richard looked around.

"I suppose you're disgusted with me."

He shot me a perplexed look. "With you? No." He examined a golden tray. "I'm disgusted with the earl. All these people in power are just the same. They aren't constricted by the rules of human decency."

"Your rules really are too constricting."

"He took advantage of you." He crossed his arms and faced me. "Did you like kissing him?"

"I think what I liked was having you watch."

"What!"

"This is how I am, Richard. The true Kali. I went away for a long time after working in the brothel, but now I'm finding my old self again. I can share my love easily with a man or a woman. The gender makes no difference to me, only the person."

He eyed me a while and then tipped up his nose. "It's fine for you to be that way, Kali. That's the nature of your people. I've no right to criticize a foreigner who's only known one way of life. I know you're a good person. But let me put things to you this way. If that earl learned of a homosexual in his city he would have him burned to death. He's a hypocrite, and that's worst thing any man can be."

My face crinkled with revulsion. "Is that true?"

"He named the man who makes and enforces the laws. I'm sure Easton is the same as everywhere else, if it wasn't I would have heard about it. Even if he's not condemning men himself he's authorizing the men who do. And yet he's

asking you into his bed, right in front of a stranger, as though no one can touch him."

"I'm sorry. I'm still learning how corrupt your world is."

He paced to the other side of the room. "It's corrupt all right."

"What should I do? He will press things with me."

"Damn it, Kali, if I'd known he was such a deviant—"

"Watch your words."

"Sorry, hypocrite who would try to pull you into his bed, then I wouldn't have sought this audience. I expected the earl to be an absolute pillar of a man." He shook his head derisively. "I made a mistake."

"Would you mind if I just slept with him? I think things would be easier that way."

"Of course I would mind!" Richard's voice cracked with emotion.

That was the first time I became sure there was something between us. The conviction in his voice was not that of a protector, but of a jealous lover. Richard didn't see this then. He acted with emotion and not thought. But I saw, and I knew.

"Then I won't sleep with him. I won't sleep with anyone."

He swallowed.

"But if you want to stay on good terms with this earl, you have to let me flirt and play without holding back. Otherwise he's going to become your enemy."

He leaned back his head. "Yes. Right. That's how it has to be. I didn't know what I was getting into, and now you have to suffer."

"I won't suffer. Your feelings are the only thing that upset me. I wish you could have fun."

He fixed a gaze onto me.

Two tailors came into the room pushing wheeled wardrobes.

"Why don't you get drunk and flirt with the women?" I stood so the man could measure me. "Maisie's done worse to you. You should take this opportunity to get rid of some stress."

"That's true. I don't owe her anything anymore."

I grinned. "Have fun, Richard."

28 The Soiree

Richard was dressed in a long black waistcoat with tails, white tunic, and knee-length leather boots. He insisted he keep the outfit and got no protests from the tailors. They made me a new silk loincloth that left more of my buttocks exposed and a belt with hanging chains. Then my tunic was removed, and a jeweled choker went around my neck. I looked like a seductress.

I posed while held in Richard's gaze. "What do you think?"

"I think you're going to get cold. How…how about a…a uh…shirt."

I blinked at him. His face had gone red. I turned away so I could beam with a triumphant smile.

We were brought to a grand set of stairs that led downward into the ballroom. I clutched Richard's arm on the mezzanine before we appeared to the crowd.

"Shall we?"

He crooked his arm to escort me, like the suave gentleman he was.

We went to the top of the stairs and the earl who was reclining on a couch with a gaggle of nobles, popped up and pointed at me.

"There he is my friends! A true faun from the land of Faunernatia!"

The well-dressed crowd faced me and applauded as we descended.

"Faunernatia?" I said.

"He can get away with anything."

We drank. We schmoozed. I answered questions and let my legs, tail, and horns get groped to everyone's satisfaction. Richard made nice with a group of women whose nipples peeked out from their bustiers. I was asked to dance by a young women and then cut in by the earl. This was toward the end of the evening when prostitutes and male dandies wandered through the ballroom with breasts or buttocks exposed.

The earl danced me into a private bedroom. He pounced on me upon the bed.

"Oh, let me make love to you. If I don't have you, I'll die."

I pouted. "I promised Richard I wouldn't."

His hands squirmed over my bare chest. "What does he have to say about it? What is he, in love with you?"

"I'm in love with him."

The earl laughed and then sealed my mouth with a deep kiss. "Well, we won't tell him."

I felt in an impossible situation. The only way to subvert him would have been to throw him off me. We would make an enemy out of him, even after all this. I didn't want to break my word to Richard, but was trapped. I vowed to admit my sin later, should we ever become a couple. (And I just did so by writing it here and letting him read this chapter.)

I tickled the side of his neck. "Would you give me that pretty pink carriage with the large cab we came in on? We're short a wagon and it would make Richard so happy."

"You want a carriage?" He put his hand into my loincloth. "I'll give you a better carriage than that."

We 'had sex' in a really stupid way. He got my cock out, pulled out his, poured oil on both organs and then humped his body against mine. Our members rubbed together until he ejaculated (I didn't). Then he kissed me with his wetness between us until he rolled over to fall asleep. I cleaned myself and returned to the party.

The debauchery had multiplied in my short absence. People were having sex on couches, or streaking naked while being chased. The two women I found Richard with were now fully bare-breasted with their skirts unhooked from their dresses. Both were dancing their fingers up and down him.

It would have sickened me if Richard had sex with either of them in this public ballroom. I clopped over and plucked him out of their arms.

"Thank you," he whispered. "Let's go back to that room they had us in."

We sneaked back up the stairs and into the bedroom. Richard latched the door shut. He plopped himself backwards on the bed with a groan.

"I take everything I said about human's being moral."

I sat near him. "You didn't have any fun?"

He grinned. "I'm drunk, Kali. Drunk on the earl's two pence. I can't complain."

I felt his shoulder. "I won't complain either."

His eyes narrowed at me. "I think you're trying to seduce me. You fancy me."

I gazed at him gently without refuting his words.

"You keep that little faun cock tucked in your panties, boy."

I laughed. "Well I'm not sleeping on the floor and there's only one bed."

Richard belched and sat up. "All right. I guess we're sharing, but no cuddling. I'm not that drunk, damn you."

He got up and stripped to his shorts. I took off the belt and crawled onto the soft mattress. Richard shook and bounced the bed to get in beside me.

"I hope I don't end up thinking your Maisie in the middle of the night."

"I wouldn't mind," I said softly.

"I'm sure you wouldn't, you little faun tart."

I laughed again because there was no malice in his voice, only playfulness.

"Hey, um, I meant to ask you, you said something about being robbed and not having any family. What was that all about?"

I turned to face him. "My only family was a step-father who died while I was finishing school. I had grandparents on my mother's side, but they disowned me because I chose to live with my step-father over them. When my step-father died, they were able to take my home away from me. I was graduating without a job or a place to live. I'd decided I wanted to be a teacher but couldn't afford the tuition. A friend made arrangements for me to get a live-in job far on the other side of our land. I was working at an inn as a prostitute for centeri men."

"Hm."

"I hated that job, Richard. It was being used over and over without any feeling behind it. No love. But, it was temporary. I was just working for my tuition for school. After a year I had enough money and was ready to head home. But I got lost,

then someone bashed my head and robbed me." I drew a breath. "All that money I suffered for all year was stolen. My whole life was ruined in a blink of an eye."

"That's horrible."

"And I just wandered. I went through the woods next to Calico, the centerus land where I'd worked, and hiked for two days. Then I found a waterfall that looked like it had a cave behind it. I went through to the path that led me to the other side of the mountains. That's when I came to your group."

He propped himself up on one arm to look at me. "All that happened right before you found us?"

I nodded. "I was in the darkest place of my life when I approached you."

His hand rubbed over his face. "My God. And so were we. We thought we would hang, or at least get hunted." He shook his head amazed. "And then we found each other. It's providence, Kali. I'm certain of it."

I smiled. "So am I."

It felt right to share a bed with him. I hoped he would realize that as well. And yes, I know he had a wife, but she'd been unfaithful. Why should he remain faithful in such a situation?

I would have made love to him that night without a stitch of guilt if he had let me.

29 The Wagon

The next day the same smooth-faced man who fetched us brought us out of the castle. In the circular drive was a weather-beaten grey wagon, with at least one rotten board, being pulled by a single mule.

"His Excellency has bestowed this most generous gift of wagon and mule to you, with his compliments."

I was outraged. What was this broken down piece of—

"It's magnificent!" Richard said with his eyes glimmering. "Thank the good earl for us! Thank him a thousand times!"

The man bowed to us. "And do come to call the next time you're in town."

"We will!"

Richard bounded down the steps to our wagon. I slowly followed. He grabbed me and hugged me off my feet when I reached him.

"You did this, didn't you? Didn't you, you little minx!"

"I did," I said with a scowl, "but I asked for that pink wagon he brought us in."

He laughed. "But this one's better. We can turn it into a proper caravan."

I folded his black cloak over me so I could join him in the driver's seat. "I had to let the earl rub against me for him to give us this. You don't mind, do you?"

He frowned a moment. "Did it upset you?"

"I didn't care, Richard."

"Then I'll be happy. You've blessed this carnival once again, Kali. I'm so grateful."

"Good. When you're happy, so am I."

His voice turned tearful suddenly. "Because I'm going to kick that treacherous witch out of our wagon and make her go live with her repulsive strong man."

My eyes widened.

"I'm divorcing her." A tear streaked down one of his cheeks. "This will be the end of it. All I needed was a place to put her. And Callum can have her if he wants. She's worthless to me now."

I placed a hand on his arm. "I'm sorry, Richard."

"So am I." He snuffled. "We were happy, Kali. I was good to her. I doted on her!"

"I know."

"But she had so little respect for me. She acted as though I should condone her cheating because I couldn't get her pregnant. As though I should just turn the other way. How could I? How can I share a bed with a woman who reeks of another man's seed?"

He vented all through the ride back, letting his volcano of emotion gush free, and achieving a sort of catharsis. When we got back to the camp which was fully packed and ready to leave, his resolve was unwavering. He went to Duncan's wagon and called out Callum. They went into the body of the new wagon and spoke without yelling because I couldn't hear them from outside.

Maisie came out of our wagon with her face white. "What's that all about? What are they talking about?"

I said nothing.

"Is that a new wagon?"

"Looks it," Duncan said to her. "Bit beat up, but it could work. I'm guessing he's giving it to Callum."

She pursed her lips. "Is that all he's doing? Why are they talking so long?"

Richard exited and strode for Maisie. Callum pulled a crate lashed to the outside of Duncan's wagon and carried it into the new one.

Duncan spat. "Yep. He's giving it to Callum."

Fergus said something to him with his hands. Duncan shrugged back at him.

"Come inside with me, Maisie," Richard said to her. "We need to talk."

She looked horrified and hesitated to follow him. She tried to get them to speak with the door open, but Richard reached beside her to slam it shut.

They were quiet in the beginning, but then shouting started. It was anger mingled with tears, and vicious enough to finish tearing apart their four year marriage. Callum stopped moving his things to stand with us and stare at their wagon.

"Holy shit," he muttered.

"Well, you knew it was coming," Duncan said with the start of a sneer.

"Yeah." Callum snorted without looking away from the wagon. "I told him she threw herself at me and he says, 'and you caught her.'"

Duncan laughed.

"And I think he's going to kick her out to live in this new wagon with me."

"Is that what you want?" Duncan said.

He shrugged. "Sure, I could take her. She's got a nice pussy. She's annoying though. Got a big mouth. Richard didn't know how to shut her up that's why she goes running off with other men. If

she goes with me, then she'll shut up and she won't think about fucking no one but me."

It sounded as though he intended on beating her. I didn't have any compassion. I felt she'd brought it on herself. Things rarely work out prettily in divorce, I'd learn.

"But why can't you forgive me?" we heard Maisie scream from the wagon.

Richard's deeper voice was harder to decipher. We all stood staring, trying to catch what stray words we could. Eventually Callum waved off the scene and continued moving.

"Hey, buddy," he said to Duncan. "Help me move my fucking bed out of here."

They pulled out a bed that was big enough for two. I imagined the new wagon would work for them. I pitied the mule who had to pull Callum's huge body without any help. (Though later I learned a mule is stronger than a horse, and would have no trouble).

Maisie came out of the wagon red-faced and ran into Callum's arms.

"He threw me away. He threw me away! Oh, Callum!"

He squeezed her. "That's okay, baby, I got you."

Richard pushed a chest out of the door of the wagon. It broke open revealing Maisie's purple tent.

"Be careful, you ass!" Maisie said.

Callum hoisted it on his shoulder. The next few minutes was filled with Richard throwing out Maisie's stuff and Callum moving it to their wagon.

Then everyone was where they should be. The new equilibrium was established.

30 The Confession

We mounted our respective wagons and headed out of the city.

At our midday break everyone sat on the grass in a group. Callum, Richard, Maisie, Duncan, Fergus, and me, and Richard passed out almond cookies.

"Nice, thank you," Callum said to him.

"You're welcome," Richard said.

"Oh, how sweet they are," Maisie said to Callum.

"You like that, baby?"

She smiled to him. "Mm-hm.

Richard eyed them a moment, but then snuffled and looked out at the horses.

Duncan climbed to his feet with a disgusted expression. "Well this is weird as fuck." He went back into his wagon.

Richard sighed and headed to his. I came in to find him sorting things. We had a much wider space in the middle now. He turned to me.

"Why don't we make you a bed on top of these crates?"

"I'm fine on the bench."

"You sure?"

I nodded. "Are you all right, Richard?"

He looked toward the ceiling. "No, Kali, I'd say I'm pretty far from all right."

I felt tears build behind my eyes. He looked at me with a thin smile.

"But I will be. In time."

I clutched his shoulder.

He grinned with more effort. "And I didn't lose my strong man."

"No, you didn't. You handled things perfectly."

"I handled things like a good businessman. And I'll continue that way. Callum doesn't have to know how much I want to kill him."

"I think he knows."

He laughed. "Well he'd have to be an idiot not to."

Well continued on to the village of Strawberry. Children cooed and screamed at our colorful new banners, but audiences were less than a dozen at a time. We stayed only two days and then packed up. Next was Trentby, which had a lake in the center. We set up on the bank to much larger crowds. After the last show Richard plucked me out of the wagon and forced me to skinny dip with him and Fergus. I saw Richard laugh and believed he was coming out of the other side of his misery.

These two shows went so smooth you'd think nothing changed. The only difference was that Maisie went to bed with Callum instead of Richard. It all became normal to us so quickly.

I found out Maisie no longer shared half her take with the pot. She kept all her half-pennies as her only income, which was substantial. Richard didn't fight about it. I knew he wished to withdraw from her and Callum as much as he could.

Onward to Calixco, the first town without a wall, only the remnants of one that had crumbled. While looking down on the town from the hillside I finally asked Richard why the towns had walls.

"The country was divided once without a single king to rule over all of us. Men would conquer a city and then put up a wall so they could keep it. This was a long time though. There is no reason for the walls now."

After Calixco we were fully within a territory without walls, and traffic increased. I had to wear Richard's cloak when I sat with him on the driver's seat and pull on my hood whenever a passer drew near.

"You know, this year it's fine for you to keep your act as it is, but when we start over again, start going round to the same villages a second time with you, you have to come up with a new routine."

I balked where I sat beside him. "What? I have to memorize a new poem?"

"I pick a new section of verses every year so that no onlooker has ever heard the same parable twice, but for you I want something more. I'd like to have you do an act on the main stage in this cloak, just teasing at what might be beneath it, before you go to Duncan's stage and take the cloak off."

I groaned. "Richard, I'm not an actor."

He scowled at me. "That's horseshit, Kali. Stop pretending to be modest. I've heard your show a dozen times. You glow on the stage. You can't tell me you don't love it. You drink in all the reactions of the crowd, getting bigger and bigger as you go. I'd say you're just as good as I am."

"No I'm not."

"You are! What you lack in finesse you make up with your beauty."

I blushed. "Oh, Richard."

"Kali, I could make a whole show just with the two of us. Half a play, and half a carnival with a faun. We'd be magnificent on the stage together. You could take the female roles against me. We'd have them wailing in their seats."

"It's alright for me to play a woman when I'm a man?"

"Oh yes, don't worry about that. It's common. Women aren't supposed to be actors. It's unseemly. All the plays have younger men play the women."

"And do they kiss them?"

"Yes. It's acting. It's allowed. Not disgusting kisses like what you gave the earl, but pecks."

"Your world is so full of contradiction, Richard. You say men who lie with men get burned alive, and yet men kissing men on stage is fine. And all your royalty thinks it's fine too. It's as if the commoners have been forced to wear horse blinders."

"Nicely put."

"Do you still think it's abhorrent for a man to love another man?"

"Not for you, Kali, I told you. You're not from our world. I can't impose our values on you."

"Hmph." I thought a moment. "Is it all right for me to impose my values on you?"

He grinned. "Oh, you'll try. You'll certainly try."

My heart began to race. "Richard, in all seriousness, I like you, and not just as a friend."

His brow rose, and he turned to me. "Not one for subtlety, are you?"

I lowered my head and swallowed.

"For your information I already knew. And frankly, that's your problem. I have enough to deal with as it is."

"I wasn't trying to trouble you, Richard."

He focused on the road for a while. "I like you too much to be troubled by your infatuation. But make a promise to me right now."

I glanced at him. He did not meet my eyes.

"You must swear you will not leave the carnival, even if I never reciprocate your feelings."

I managed a half-smile only because I didn't believe him. "I have no where to go, Richard."

"Oh, unfortunately you do. That earl would be happy to make you an ornament in his disgusting court."

"That's not the sort of life I want to have."

He looked at me. "I'm glad to hear it."

We were quiet after that, but I felt so much more needed to be said. I wanted some hope from him. Some sign he acknowledged feelings for me, even if he never intended on acting on them.

I was left with nothing.

31 Rain

In Dursby transients had taken over the square where we were supposed to set up our act. We lost half a day pushing out their shantytown, so we'd have room. Then there wasn't enough space for our audience, and less than seven people came to the first show. Richard gave up and ordered we tear down. We couldn't even spend the night with our props set up because thieves were all around us.

"Let me beat all these fuckers out of here!" Callum said over our communal dinner.

"There's no point. The people know the square was taken over by vagrants. They won't come out here. They're scared of getting robbed."

"I'm scared of getting robbed!" Duncan said. "Let's get the fuck out of here."

"At dawn. If we leave at night, we'll definitely get robbed."

"Fuck this, I'm going to bed!" Callum got up and snatched Maisie by the arm making her dump her bread on the ground.

"Ow! Damn it! You made me spill my bread!"

"Shut the fuck up! I said we're going to bed!"

She crouched down to retrieve her loaf, brushing the dirt from it as she followed.

I noticed she had a bruise in the same place Callum grabbed her.

When his wagon shut, Richard pointed his nose at the door.

"What am I supposed to do about that?"

"Nothing," Duncan said.

"And what if he beats her?"

"She's got enough spine to get away from him."

Richard fumed.

"What?" Duncan said. "You want her back?"

"No. I want her away from him."

I awoke the next morning to Callum stomping a vagrant. My poster was rolled up in his hand. He'd saved it from being stolen and I was grateful. It was a relief to leave that town.

Applewaithe had no vagrants in the square, but pouring rain started and didn't stop for two days. Richard left us parked without setting up. It was pointless to get our props wet because no one would come out in the rain.

After that it was muddy and Richard said we had to wait another day for the sun to come out.

"Are we going to miss the festival in the capital?" Duncan said.

"We're on schedule," Richard said. "We shaved a day off Strawberry and four days off Dursby."

There was a tavern within walking distance. Callum and Maisie were the first to traverse the mud to get to it. The next day Duncan and Fergus went. On the day after the rain stopped Richard went. He came back minutes later.

"Get my cloak on and come to the tavern. There's no one in there."

I was restless and happy to get out. The only ones in the tavern were the barkeep and our crew. Richard had me reveal myself to our server, so we didn't appear suspicious. He'd seen the poster so wasn't completely surprised. We settled into a corner table to drink ale while a piano magically played by itself. The rest of our group

stayed at the bar. We had no fear of leaving the wagons alone since all the doors had locks and we hadn't yet set up.

Richard watched Maisie at the bar. Callum was bragging to Duncan while she sat with her head down, cupping both sides of her glass with her hands.

"I can't help feeling responsible for her."

I eyed him.

"What can I do?"

"You sacrificed everything not to lose your strong man. If you interfere now, it will be for nothing."

"But she doesn't deserve to be mistreated, even if she did betray me. She's a tiny girl, and he's a gigantic beast."

"I don't think he's hitting her."

"It's a matter of time, Kali." He drew a long breath. "He could kill her. Wouldn't that be on my conscience?"

I kept my lips sealed. The selfish part of me was jealous that he still cared for her. The rational part tried to be a comforting friend.

"Give him a warning."

He looked at me.

"Let him know you're still keeping watch over her."

"You're right. I'll talk to him."

If the talk happened in Applewaithe I was not aware of it. We set up that night and started our show the next day. The sun was out. The crowds were good. We got back on track and spirits lifted.

32 The Capital

Traffic increased tenfold as we approached the capital. There was no place to camp on the sides of the road, so we drove the horses all day. When the massive city appeared ahead of us, the road shot off into tributaries. Richard led us down one such side road to escape traffic and take a break on the grass. The group huddled for a meeting.

"I'm going to take Kali to the castle and see if we can get an audience with the king. The earl has sent word by now, I'm sure. If we get the king's blessing we can have our show right in the front yard of the castle."

"How long are we going to have to wait while you're trying to kiss the king's ass?" Callum said.

"However long will be worth it. We won't be a side act this year. We're the main event."

Richard had me ride behind him on the back of our fittest horse. I had to clutch him around the belly to stay on. It was good he wasn't bothered by my infatuation because this was as close as two men could ever be.

We rode down wide cobble streets that would put Easton to shame. Buildings three stories high towered around us made of immaculately painted wood and thatched roofs. There was space on the sides of the roads for people to walk, and traffic flowed easily in both directions.

It was a half hour ride through the city and then we reached a large park. Dozens of carnivals were spaced throughout it. Some were one wagon affairs, and others massive companies with a half

dozen wagons covered in paintings of their attractions. A few were not wagons at all, but tents that were brought in on the backs of horses. These venues were more shops than shows, selling trinkets, ribbons, sugary treats or skewered meat. The further we traveled the more crowded it became. We had to skirt a large clump of wagons before coming out of the other side of the park. There we hit smack into the castle which was so high its spires went into the clouds.

A stone path bisected two areas of greenery leading to an iron gate. Richard pointed to one expansive side of level grass.

"We'll set up here." He gestured to the other side. "The horses and Callum's wagon can go over here."

"You really think they'll allow that?" I noticed no other troupe dared to spill onto the street leading to the castle.

"We can ask."

The iron gate was decorated with black metal vines and had spears on top. It had to be seven feet high. Two guards with partisans and puffy red and blue tunics stood at the door.

"Good afternoon," Richard said to one of them.

He gave no response, either in expression or words.

"His majesty received word from the Earl Chantwell of Easton that we would seek an audience with him." Richard pulled my in front of him by my shoulders. He took the cloak off me. "This is Kali. A half man half sheep from a village beyond the death cliffs called Schaletar."

The two guards remained stone-faced a moment more, then their lips parted as they looked up and down me.

"Is he real?" one of them said. "You know its death to defraud the king."

"He is real," Richard said calmly. "So I have no fear of death."

They exchanged a look at each other. "Well, such a creature is an attraction, certainly, but what makes you think our king would have time for him? Go on about your show, carney, and cease troubling us."

"My good sirs," Richard said, as sweetly and humbly as I've ever seen him. "The Earl of Easton was kind enough to give us audience, and he insisted I bring such a mystical creature to our good king. He implied that if Kali here did a private show for his majesty, we might be allowed to have the place of honor on the grass in front of your gate. Surely you must understand why I pursue this. It's not my intent to cause any trouble."

The guard walked to the brick pillar beside the gate and swung a lever to unlock it. He snatched me by my arm and pulled me in, then bashed Richard in the chest when he tried to follow.

"Just him. Not you. Wait here."

I shot him back a frightened look.

"It's all right, Kali! Be your charming self and make sure the king knows what we want."

"I still don't think the king will make time for you," the guard pulling me said. "But that's up to his minister."

I was brought to a head guard, then a nobleman, and then entered the castle to go before a minister. Finally I received the reception Richard

had expected. The lanky man with a single pleat of brown hair dropped his jaw at the sight of me.

"Oh yes, he must be the one Chantwell wrote about."

The gate guard, who'd stayed by my side throughout my tour, said, "Indeed my lord, that's what they told me. I knew at once I should take such an amazing creature to you directly."

The minister bent my legs and tugged my tail and horns. Then he barraged me with the same questions I'd gotten in Easton. Where was I from? Were there more of me? What did I want?

I answered honestly, winning him over in the same way I had the earl.

In an hour's time I was brought to a throne room where the elderly king sat. There was no throne for a queen, so I presumed him a widower. He reached out with arthritic fingers and made me sit on his lap. The man was feeble and had a goiter. He cuddled me as one might do a puppy. I endured all his fawning with good humor. The minister was still with us. I looked down from our throne at him.

"Is it possible we might set up our carnival on the grass before the gate? I'm told it's a place of honor. Would it be too brazen of me to presume I'm worthy?"

"Not at all! The space shall be yours."

Hooray!

The king seemed to think this marked the end of our meeting. He let me free and muttered something to his attendant beside him.

"He would like you to attend the celebration here after the festival."

I bowed deeply. "Of course. It would be a pleasure."

By the time I got back to Richard it was dark out. He ran to the gate to meet me. The minister had walked me out.

"You have permission to take this place before the gate. See too it you don't block the walkway."

"Absolutely. Thank you, thank you!"

With that, we went back to our horse. Richard gave me a kiss on my cheek.

"Good work."

I gave a shallow nod while blushing.

"It was nothing."

33 The Gem of the Festival

The other carnival masters were quick to tell us we weren't allowed to set up in that sacred place. Richard was smug to most of them due to bad blood in their past. Many went to the guards at the gate to tell on us. They had to walk away with their tails between their legs. We were the jewel of the festival to the ire of them all.

Merely being in that spot lured the massive crowds toward us. They filled the grass and the street beyond it to watch both our stages. Word soon spread about the real life faun you could actually touch. Richard had us doing five shows a day.

During Fergus' acrobatics Richard came back to my wagon to let in an eager young reporter named Colby and his sketch artist. I gave my first interview to the King's Papers. The artist drew studies of my horns, legs, and tail, as I answered questions. This went on a long while, so I had to interrupt him when it came time for my act. At our carnival there were both peasants and nobles. All were eager to give their pennies to touch me.

On the last day of the show we were overwhelmed by crowds too large to handle. The paper had gone out and everyone in the capital wanted to see me. Some even booed the main stage act demanding to see the faun. Richard had our shows run one after the other all day. By midnight we had to turn away a hundred more late-comers.

Richard collapsed in his bed, flush with coin but exhausted.

"Thank God the festival is over."

I crawled onto his bed and reclined beside him. "The king wants me at his after-festival celebration."

"I know. You told me."

"Are we going?"

He opened his eyes. "Of course we're going. You can't say no to the king."

I smiled.

Richard threw a pillow at me. "Now get the hell off my bed, you seducer."

I ran away with laughter.

A guard came out to tell us the king wanted our entire carnival inside the courtyard for us to give our show to his guests. We frantically tore down and then just as frantically set up on the high porch attached to the back of the castle. Servants took our horses and mule so we became stranded there.

At dusk we gave our show for the delighted nobles and royalty. I was made to walk through them letting them all feel me and question me. This was the sort of celebration Richard expected the royalty to have. There were no bare bosoms or bottoms.

We drank, we feasted, we mingled. Then a servant said we had rooms for the night. We followed him into a corridor where numerous guests were staying. People fucked with open doors, and the topless women were running through the hall.

Richard became stoic. "Here we are."

We separated into three rooms and locked the doors. The halls were a riot of noise all night. We both slept with our heads beneath the pillows.

The next morning we tried to escape while the other guests slept off their carousing. A page arranged for our animals to be returned to us. We

tore down and slowly rode for the gate. The king's minister stopped us on the way out.

"His majesty thanks you for your performance." We were handed a heavy satchel of money. "He hopes you'll visit again during the next festival."

All the weariness disappeared from Richard's face. He beamed a gigantic smile.

"We shall indeed!"

34 Division

The festival was where I began to come into my fame. I shall always remember how happy and excited we were through that exhausting week. There was no time for strife between us because we were all busy doing what we did best and making a kingly sum of money while we were at it.

The next town we were going to was Maisie's home.

It was fifty miles out of the capital, and so a half dozen other carnivals also went there. Richard claimed there wasn't room in the square for us without bothering to check. We parked our three wagons behind an inn, paying a tenpence for the privilege.

After sleeping off a day of travel we each slowly emerged to breakfast. We were flush with provisions after visiting a grocer in the capital.

"You'll come with me to the Peace's Justice after we're done eating, Maisie," Richard said.

Her eyes narrowed. "For an annulment. Not a divorce."

"He won't give us an annulment."

She lifted her nose. "Well, I'm not getting a divorce. My father has to live in this town."

I saw a glint of evil in Richard's eyes. "Okay. We'll ask for an annulment."

Callum gave a knowing laugh.

"Are you going to marry her, Callum?" Richard asked.

He sneered. "Who said anything about fucking marriage?"

"I can't have an unwed woman in my troupe."

"Why the fuck not?"

Richard stood. "Ready, Maisie?"

She got up and dusted off her skirt. "Fine. Let's go."

Callum bolted up. "I'm going too."

"To have the Peace's Justice marry you?"

"No!"

"Then sit down! This my private business and you're not welcome!" It was the first time I'd seen Richard shout.

Callum waved him off and retook his seat.

Two hours later Richard returned alone. The air lit up with tension when he appeared. It was almost palpable. I could see Richard's stern face braced for conflict.

"Where the fuck is Maisie?"

"She went home to her father."

"Fuck! Are you kidding me!" Callum rose and stomped a circle around us in anger. "Why the fuck is she gone? She's part of this carnival!"

Richard stayed focused on the camp fire.

"I'm going to her house!"

"Callum," Richard said without emotion. "Maisie knows where we are and is a grown woman. If she wants to come back to you, no one is stopping her. She's decided to go home. There's nothing you can do about that."

"The fuck there isn't!" He went into his carriage and slammed the door.

We remained quiet a moment in his wake. Duncan snuffled to break the silence.

"You divorced her?"

Richard nodded.

"She wanted to go home?"

"I talked her into it."

He rubbed his hands together to get rid of bread crumbs. "So why don't I be the fortune teller now?"

"I told her she could keep her tent and kit."

"What? What the fuck did you do that for?" Duncan rose and stomped to his wagon while swearing. Another door was slammed.

Richard put his face in his hand. While he wasn't looking Fergus slunk into the wagon with Duncan.

"It was what needed to happen," I said softly.

"I know."

In the morning Callum's wagon was gone, and a note was tacked to our door. I read it first and then gave it to Richard.

This shit was never going to work out. You threw her away but can't stand another man to have her. You're pathetic. I'm through with wiping your ass.

He took a deep sigh. Outside we faced Duncan's folded arms and angry face.

"So what the fuck are we going to do now?"

Richard groaned and relit our fire. "You'll have to do a clown magic act where his strong man act was. I'll get you a kit and we'll run through a routine."

"No," Duncan said.

The two stared at each other.

Duncan's lower lip trembled. "I told you from the start, I ain't got no talent, and I ain't going to be a fucking clown. I'm going back to the capital and going to find me some work."

Richard's gaze was clear, but I sensed him unraveling. "Take one of the horses from your wagon and go."

Duncan shook his head. "It's my wagon."

"Leave me Fergus!"

He shook his head again. Fergus stuck his body out of the door at the sound of his name. He looked at the empty space where Callum's wagon had been and put his hand on his mouth.

Duncan looked at him. "We're going, Fergus. Callum's gone and there ain't no act left."

"Of course there's an act. We were the gem of the festival!"

"Not we." Duncan jabbed a finger at me. "It."

Richard's jaw tightened.

Fergus got out of the wagon and signed something to Richard.

"We'll find another actor. It's easy enough."

He signed again.

"No you're not. You could keep going into your forties."

Fergus shook his head and signed some more.

"Just stay for as long as it takes for me to build the troupe back up."

"Come on, Fergus!" Duncan said from the driver's seat of his wagon.

Fergus shook his head at Richard and left. Their wagon pulled out of the lot.

Richard was shaking beside me. He went back into his wagon and closed the door. I didn't dare follow. What could I possibly say? We were at our peak just a day ago, and now we'd been torn apart. I sat beside the fire wrapped in his cloak.

Richard emerged in the afternoon. I peeked up at him. He gave me a soft smile.

"Let's get out of this town."

35 The Play

On our way out we saw Callum sitting at the fire with another carnival in the square. Richard sneered at him.

"That's a three pence show. Even with him."

"With him it goes down to two pence." Richard laughed.

We had planned on going to a southern village named Snakeberry. I saw we were headed back to the capital instead.

"What are you thinking, Richard?"

"We don't have a carnival anymore. We have a two-person play." He glanced at me. "A play should be in a theater where the crowds come to us from here on."

I wanted to mention we didn't have a play, but he was being positive. I had to be as well.

"We don't need them, Kali. Callum was a bastard, Maisie was devious, Fergus was great, but came as a package with his asshole father. The two of us are the best thing in this show. We're better than transients. We should be the toast of the capital."

"So the plan you had before, about you and me in a play…"

"We're doing that."

I gave a shuddering sigh. "Can we take a break first? We have money, don't we?"

He turned to me and grinned. "Sure. We'll rent a room for a month in the heart of the city. How does that sound?"

"Sounds nice."

He took my hand. "It's just you and me now, Kali. We'll make it, just the two of us."

I placed my hand over his. "I prefer it this way."

Richard and I pooled our funds and had 230 pounds. We found a space in the arts district, walking distance from the theater, but with only one bed. Richard talked about selling the wagon, but didn't proceed. We both were uncertain about the future.

He brought in his books and found us a play about a princess posing as a commoner who fell in love with a rogue. It was a lovely concept because the princess kept hidden in a cloak until the end of the play. The only trouble was there were seven parts in addition to ours.

"That's no trouble at all. The theater will help us hire actors for all the parts."

"What theater?"

He took me to our large window and pointed to a building with a grand marble facade. "That one."

I watched hundreds of people filing in for a show. It shouldn't have daunted me, since I'd performed before large crowds before, but it somehow did.

"What makes you so sure?"

Richard tugged my tail. "You make me sure, Kali." He forgot himself and drew close to me. "You open all the doors for me."

"Arc you being the seducer now?"

He grinned and stepped away. "Sorry."

We read the play while sitting side by side on the edge of the bed. I did all of Jawlee's lines and Richard did Morco's and all the other characters. Three times in the play Jawlee and

Morco kissed. Richard was reading his character with such passion my heart fluttered during every tender scene.

For our next read through Richard had us get up and act it out, with him still holding the book to read our lines. He was now not only most of the characters but the director as well. He described the sets to me, dictated my body language, mood, and delivery. I became infected with his vision. This would be a magnificent play.

He placed his arm around me when we came to the first tender scene. My character was supposed to be swooning. I tell you, this was not hard. He looked into my eyes while delivering a speech that put a quiver in my breath.

Then he kissed me. He claimed the kiss would be a peck, but this was not a peck. He pressed his warm lips against mine, joined us in a moment of bliss, then parted to say his final line.

When he let me go, I flopped to the floor. My legs had lost all their strength.

"Kali! Get a hold of yourself."

I tried to crawl up. I was an idiot. The kiss had not been real.

He lifted me by one arm. "Are you all right?"

I wasn't all right. "Let's continue," I said.

His face strained and then he turned away. "No, let's take a break." He walked over to the bed and sat. "This seems like a cruel play to tackle considering your feelings for me."

I stepped in front of him, still shaken. "My feelings are my problem."

Again, anguish flickered across his face. "What do you want me to do, Kali?"

"Nothing. I've never made any demands."

"But I don't want to hurt you."

I gave him an angry smile. "I think you're the one hurting. That's why you won't drop it."

A grunt came up deep from his throat that confirmed my words. "I care about you."

I smiled. "I know." I plucked up the playbook. "Let's continue."

36 Starting Over

We memorized the first act of the play and performed in our rented room without aid of the book. Richard coached me to perfection. I might truly have been his equal now. The kissing became easier, but always put thunder in my chest. I focused on realizing his dream rather than indulging in my desires.

Our wagon was parked under the apartment in a tight bay. Richard peeled the poster of me off it and went to the theater. I watched him walking down the street to the forbidding building while praying to every god I knew. An hour later he returned.

The weather had gone chilly now as autumn approached. Richard wore his stage coat to keep warm. He pulled it off in our doorway.

"The manager didn't have much time to talk to me. The poster helped. I told him we wanted to put on Midwinter Love. He said if I have a faun playing Jawlee I have to rewrite the verses so it makes sense. We'll have to add in a poem about her strange birth and say that this is why she wears the cloak."

"Perhaps her family was hiding her because they thought her a freak."

"Right, right! And Morco's the only one she reveals herself to."

"That's all we have to do to have our play run there?"

"No. I didn't get that far. He has this season fully booked, and next season is almost full as well."

I became crestfallen. "Oh."

"He said to come back tomorrow morning to discuss things further."

"I thought we would be the only show for at least a year. That we'd have two shows a day, and one day a week dark."

He sat on the bed. "That's what I thought as well. Kali, I'm new to this business. It will take time to figure out how it all works."

I took his hand. "We have time."

The next morning Richard brought the manager back to our room so he could look at me. He was a squat man with a pronounced forehead.

"Well, he's certainly a draw, your faun here," the man said, perched on our only spare chair of the room. "That's if you can get the word out."

"I've never had trouble drawing crowds to a show," Richard said.

"The theater is fifty pounds a night to rent. I usually take this out of ticket sales. If you want to book an open slots, I need the payment up front. You're not a proven company to us yet. After you're established we can proceed as normal. Now, do you have your set, your props, your costumes, and your acting troupe?"

Richard and I stared at him blankly.

"Good, sir, all I have is the world's only faun."

"And that's a draw, like I said, but he can't just stand on the stage and do nothing. You must have a proper show. These things cost money. How much do you have?"

"Enough to produce an exceptional show."

"Well good luck to you then." He got up. "If you want to book the theater my first date is in September. Come to the box office tomorrow with a ten pound deposit."

"I will. I'll see you then."

He left, and I flopped back on our bed with a groan. "This sounds impossible."

Richard sat next to me and soothed my thigh. "It's not impossible. I've put on shows before that needed all the things he mentioned. We'll make it happen here, too."

"You're so sure of yourself."

"A man can draw great succor from a dream. My dream is to be on the stage with you, amazing the crowds. Can you imagine their reaction at the end when you drop your cloak?"

I grinned. "It's a nice dream."

"It will take all our money, Kali."

I sat up to look at him.

"If it works, we'll be wealthy again soon. We're not just actors, but the owners of the production. If we fail, well, then—we'll have to get creative. Are you willing to take the risk?"

"If we fail, we'll pull our wagon to the park and do a tiny show for two pence a ticket."

Richard laughed. "That's the spirit! Oh, how I wish I'd had you for a wife instead of Maisie. She tore apart every scheme I had out of fear of failure. Sometimes for good reason, but a few of my ideas might have been winners. With her I'd never know."

"Richard, in all regards except for the physical, I am your spouse. You do realize that don't you?"

He nodded at me. "The physical, too. We've been kissing."

This made me erupt with laughter. I wanted to hug myself against him on the bed. It would have felt so natural. But, alas, I continued to resist my desires.

Richard went to a play at the theater the next night. It cost fifty pence, but was an investment well rewarded. He managed to talk his way back stage to recruit actors and mine information. When he returned he was bursting with excitement.

"We're going to rent a studio for ten pence a day and get the show ready. I've got actors for five other parts, and they say they know some people for the rest. One man, Chance, he is an actor and a costumer. I have to go buy fabrics with him once he measures everyone. Another man says he knows a theater that did a production of Midwinter Love across town that might still have the sets stored away. I'm taking the wagon there straight away tomorrow to see what I can buy."

I became giddy. "It doesn't sound so hard now."

He sat beside me and took both my hands in his. "No, we can do this. I already put ten pounds down for a deposit. September fourth at 7pm."

I felt the room spin. "Oh my gods, that's only three weeks away!"

"That's all we need! And once we're a huge success, we'll block off a whole season of the theater. Think of it, four hundred seats, fifty pence a head, and we only have to give the theater fifty pounds!"

I ran to the desk to make calculations with pen and paper. The reality of the math deflated me. "We would have to sell 100 seats just to pay for the theater."

He came behind me and put his hands on my shoulders. "Yes. But we're going to sell out. Each and every night."

I calculated the best case scenario while thinking Maisie might have been right about

Richard's scheme's. The theater was taking a tremendous cut.

"If we sell out, it's two hundred pounds. Fifty goes to the theater. How much will you pay your actors?"

"One pound a show should do it."

"What about now, when they're rehearsing for you?"

"Hm."

"And what will the costumes and sets cost?"

"If they're too much, I'll come up with alternatives."

"Remember at the festival? Our largest crowd was scarcely two hundred people. How are we going to get four hundred to come to this show?"

He pointed a finger at me. "That reporter, Colby. I'll get you another interview with him."

I nodded. "That's a good idea."

"And you have a point. Our budget should be to break-even with only one show. Give me the numbers for that. I'll let it guide me. You're quite good at keeping my head screwed on."

"There's only one number. One hundred and fifty pounds. That's what you'd make if you sold out after you pay the rent for the theater."

"One hundred fifty pounds. All right. I won't go a pence over that."

I handed him the pen and paper. "Well keep track! That's almost all our money."

He took this, leaned down to hug me, and kissed my cheek. "You're exactly who I needed, Kali."

I patted his arm. "Yes, husband."

37 Preparation

They play was edited for a faun lead and I had my lines memorized by the first studio rehearsal. My presence made all the actors excited. They believed the show would be a hit just because of me.

A fellow actor the same age as me measured us all and showed sketches for our costumes. He would take ten pounds of our precious money to make us look like our fabled characters.

No money was asked for by the actors for rehearsals. We practiced the first act, showing incredible promise, and then broke for the night. Richard was gone before I woke the next morning. That was his only chance to get the sets from that other theater. The silver wooden castle, wishing well, and carriage clogged our rented room.

Richard found the office of the newspaper and got an impromptu interview for me. The reporter Colby was fascinated that I had settled there. He did a full article, mentioning the play and theater toward the end. That was two weeks before our date. One week before the play my poster had new text glued to it and was hung in the theater lobby. I watched out my window every night a crowd filed into that theater hoping they would all see the poster and mark the date.

By the third rehearsal we'd gone through the full play, though not everyone had their lines memorized. Half the time was spent being fitted into our costumes.

Richard had every line memorized the fifth time we rehearsed, giving a magnificent performance. We all did, I thought, except for one

mistake made by our costumer who played a servant. Richard insisted we were ready. That was good because the play was day after tomorrow.

We were allowed to carry our set to the theater the next day. The manager had us place everything behind rear curtains so we wouldn't disrupt the show there tonight. I was in Richard's hood which was allowed to get dusty because a different red hood was made for the show.

"You're all ready to go, right? Not just sets but actors and costumes too, right?" the manager said.

"Yes," Richard said with a gleaming smile. "We're going to be amazing."

"I hope you are, because you're sold out."

How anticlimactic! I expected to have to peer out at the audience from the stage to know if we were a success. The manager had both ruined the surprise and overjoyed me.

"Did you hear that!" Richard pulled me off my feet and spun me in a hug. "Sold out!"

I squealed with laughter. Yes, squealed. Richard sometimes made me feel like a coquette.

"Well let's get over to the office and book at least another week. If you're terrible, we won't need to go further than that, but right now I've got people coming in looking for tickets by the dozen."

"We're going to be fantastic. I'll book a whole season if you let us."

The manager backtracked. "Hold your horses! Let's see how it goes tomorrow. But I will put you in the register for October for now…if it goes well. If not I can keep the ten-pence variety show going."

38 Love

The next night came. Everything was prepared. I acted with my horns and legs hidden in my cloak until the second act. Then Richard tipped me down to kiss me and my horns were revealed. The audience cooed with a wave of awe and applauded through our kiss. That made Richard hold it longer. I quite enjoyed that.

In the last act, during our final scene, I let the cloak fall from me. The short toga dress I wore beneath it showed my hooves. My tail came through a hole in the back. Richard pulled me in his arms and kissed me with a full passionate embrace. The audience roared with cheers.

We took our bows. Richard and I got the most applause. I bowed, spun and wagged my little tail. They were enraptured.

Backstage the manager brought us our purse. Each actor got a pound and a quarter (since a pound was apparently too little for such a show). Our list of bookings was gone over. One more show this week, then a solid two weeks, and then the full month of October.

Two days after the show the King's Paper gave us a glowing review. There was some criticism over our paltry set and the acting of one servant, but the rest was positive. The article hyped the excitement of my reveal, how we teased with horns and then showed a full sheep-man at the end. My authenticity had been proven at the festival, and that made our show truly legitimate. 'The greatest marvel to come to the capital in at least a decade.'

We sold out nearly every night. Richard's instinct had been correct. We became the toast of the capital. Our riches were renewed quickly and then grew further. Money didn't matter as much to Richard as fame, but for me it was security. I stowed away our pounds in our mattress, cupboard, and nightstand.

On show days we had two sessions, the matinee would have at least 375 seats full and the night session would sell out. After such a long day we collapsed home in our bed, falling willingly into oblivion.

It was during this time I awoke to Richard spooning against my backside. His hand searched over my chest as though something was missing.

"I'm not Maisie, Richard."

He nudged up his head. "Hm? Oh." Then he drooped and went back to sleep. His body remained pressed against mine.

After that night he rolled into that position automatically as though I were his wife and not another man. I accepted this with some conflict. We were too busy to delve into the matter.

Our show lasted longer than October. We ran all winter, with Tuesdays dark, and then retired Midwinter Love in May. Summer was the start of our vacation. Another production, The General's Daughter, was on our horizon for next autumn.

For now, though, we rested.

We never gave up our room in the theater district. From there Richard and I could walk to shops and restaurants. I wore his cloak but was still recognized and harangued for the odd autograph or two. (Richard would sign his name beside mine when the people realized he was the male lead from our play.) There didn't seem to be a need to hide.

It was two days after Midwinter Love ended and Richard and I sipped coffee at an expensive café. We were at the only outdoor table. No people were close. I decided to speak the words that had floated in the air around us for so long.

"Let me make love to you, Richard." My eyes had to be filled with longing. "We're almost there, anyway. We should finish that journey."

He eyed me, sipped his coffee, then looked out onto the quiet street. "I do love you, Kali."

"Don't say 'but.' There is no reason to hold back besides your own lopsided morals. If you won't be my lover, then find a woman, marry her, and let me go."

He cringed. "That would destroy me."

I waited.

"Sex between two men...it seems so bizarre. You don't have what I need for a proper fuck."

"Richard."

He met my eyes.

"I will be the one fucking you."

He balked. "Are you kidding me?"

I remained stone faced.

"Bah. In my ass? That's going to take some whiskey." He laughed and rubbed his hand over his head. "You put it out clearly, didn't you? I was thinking of taking your behind, and pretending you were a woman. You won't let it happen that way."

I shook my head. "I'm a man. Be with me the way a man would. Accept that it isn't bizarre. It's love. My love for you. Your love for me."

Richard sighed. "Oh, Kali." He reached out and took my hand. "God, I do love you. I don't know when it happened exactly."

"I do."

"But I can't be without you. You're my dreams, my hope, my joy, wrapped into a beautiful person. My chest aches to even think of being away from you. We're just too right for each other. Like something out of a love ballad." He looked at me with his brows pulled inward. "I'm being silly aren't I?"

"No." Emotion built in my middle. "I feel the same way." And what he stated had already been clearly known to us before that moment.

That night I faced him in his embrace and kissed him the way I always wanted to. It started timid, but he took control, rolling over me and mingling our tongues. I saw something uncork in him just with the kissing. He'd realized how we were always meant to be.

When our mouths broke, he soothed my hair and traced my horns.

"Not tonight," he said. "Not the thing you mentioned."

"Something else?"

"What do you want, you sweet little faun?"

I ducked down and crawled until my mouth was level with his pelvis. Then I gently took out his cock, going slow in case he wished to stop me, and sucked him.

"Kali…" He felt my hair with both his hands.

It was divine to pleasure him, to make him grunt and buck his hips. I saw my Richard as I always wanted. When he came close to the edge, he pulled me off by my horns.

"Oh God, stop, stop!"

His body trembled with his thick organ as hard as stone. I sucked his balls and made him orgasm in my hand. He tensed and jolted. The

sounds he made, of passion built up to a tumult, rang beautifully in my ears.

I crawled back up and he kissed me without hesitation. His hand went down to my crotch to pleasure me in return. With his mouth on mine, his strong arms around me, and the taste of him on my lips…I didn't take long. He urged me with heated words, knocking me over the hard edge.

The room had a shared bath in the corridor. We sneaked out with just our loincloth and shorts on. Then we bathed together in a giant tub, soaping each other's bodies with breaks for more kissing. It was a stupid risk in this world, but we needed the intimacy to continue. We'd both found something we were unwilling to part with.

Once rinsed and dried we sneaked back into our room, two sultry thieves in the night.

39 More Love

Richard brought me to a jewel shop and covered me in baubles. They were meant for women, but he said I looked luscious in them. I felt beautiful when I saw myself in the mirror, glittering with a hundred colors.

It was my turn to pick a shop, and I chose the apothecary. I picked up lubricant. Richard groaned when he saw this and had us go to the winery. Whiskey was illegal outside of taverns, but the shopkeeper had a bottle hidden. We bought it for the princely sum of two pounds.

We had a lovely dinner at one of our favorite restaurants, flirting mercilessly with each other throughout. Richard had been so coy for so long, and now he was enthusiastic about us having sex. Human's can be so silly, pretending the obvious doesn't exist due to the brainwashing of their society. I loved that my Richard could rise above that. He was an exceptional human, and he was mine. I rejoice in that presently just as much as I did back then.

Alas, our tryst had to wait because the reporter I'd spoken to twice before was camped before our door. I don't know how he found our room, but I would guess the manager at the theater told him.

He popped to his feet when we appeared. "So you're going out into the city wearing a hood. I'd heard as much."

I lowered my hood to the man and smiled. "It doesn't seem to cause any trouble."

"I should say not! You're the toast of the city. People are in a mad fervor with gossip about

you. They wish to know how you came to trust your carnival master so much that you keep him as your constant companion."

"We're dear friends," Richard said with his arm around me.

"But how? And when? And what is life like back in the land of the fauns? May I come in? I wish to present a most fortuitous opportunity to you."

Of course we would deny nothing to the generous reviewer of Midwinter Love, particularly when we looked forward to his praise of The General's Daughter next season. Colby turned our only chair backwards and straddled it with splayed legs as Richard and I sat on our bed to face him. (The fact that our room only had one bed was not at all suspicious, for humans never presumed homosexuality among men no matter how close they seemed.)

"My publisher wants the rights to your memoir, Kali."

I blinked at him.

"The public is dying to know all about you. Tell us of your world, your childhood, your schooling, and then recount all your adventures with the carnival before you settled in our city."

"But I'm not a writer."

"Oh, he can do it," Richard said. "He's eloquent and well read. He'll give you as good a memoir as anyone."

I grew excited.

"It doesn't have to be the works of Nye. Just tell your story. We have fine editors who will make it as literate as it needs to be. If you can give us 200 pages to our satisfaction, we're prepared to pay an advance of 100 pounds, plus a five pence

royalty per book sold, paid biannually at the author's guild. What do you say? Will you give it a try?"

I thought about it and thought just made my stomach tighten. "The land of the fauns is not like that of the humans. Our customs would shock your audience."

His eyes glimmered. "The wish to be shocked."

"But I mean in terms of sexuality."

His eyes grew impossibly more luminous. "Really? Tell me!"

"He will not tell you," Richard said, "except to say that the fauns haven't our religion. What is condemned here may not be there, and thus he would implicate himself to write of it."

"Not at all. He is the darling of the king."

"Even if he's pardoned, how will society view him if they learn his values differ?"

"We are an enlightened city. The people of the capital want their world's expanded. They yearn to be challenged. To discover different values would make our Kali more fascinating. All is forgiven to foreigners. Think of the southern Morette peoples who came here decades ago. Everyone knew they were cannibals, and still their chief was made the honored guest at our parade. What can your faun tell us that would be worse than cannibalism?"

Richard stared at him in consideration.

"Perhaps this," I said. "Faun women go into estrus only once per year, and it's obvious when this condition afflicts them. Because there is no chance of pregnancy, except when a woman wishes for it, the women are as sexually free as the men. They will have sex with friends, acquaintances, or

strangers merely for the pleasure of it, without shame or criticism. This is the standard of our society."

He slapped his hands on the back of the chair. "Oh my God, Kali, I am riveted! You must tell us of this society. We're thirsty for such knowledge—desperate for it! You won't be condemned. The enlightened will envy you and the clergy will pity you."

"We'll have to think about it," Richard said.

"Think, but swear to me this." He rose a single finger in stern warning. "If you do decide to give a memoir, you'll bring it to my publishing house. Should any other house approach you, get their offer in writing and we'll match it."

I placed my hand over my heart. "I swear my story is yours, Colby. You've been too good to us for me to ever betray you."

"Magnificent!"

With that assurance he left us. I will say now that my pledge not to betray him didn't go both ways. The next King's Paper described the 'skewed values' of the fauns, repeating what I said about the women. Richard was livid, but there was no backlash. We continued to be adored in the city with even greater fascination. What the story taught me was to watch my words around the unscrupulous press. (With apologies to my publisher, but you know full well what you did.)

That night however, there was lust in my eyes. Once the nosy newsman had left, I crawled my fingers under Richard's tunic.

"Go have a bath, my love, and make your asshole clean enough for me to lick it."

He gasped in utter mortification. "My God, Kali! That's obscene."

"Correct." I attached my mouth to his neck for a buttery kiss. "I'm going to do all sorts of obscene things to you tonight."

"I'm not ready to give you what you want. Oh, you'll get it my love, in time. I see no way off this carriage ride. But not this soon. Let us build to that act in degrees."

I found a nipple below his shirt and rubbed circles over it with my finger. "Then tonight I'll make you ready." I shoved him off the bed. "Go have that bath."

He went while shaking his head. "You lewd lascivious thing."

For all my lewdness he went insane while I tongued him. I bent back his legs while he reclined on his back and tented a blanket over me with his splayed knees. He cried my name with his head thrashing, his cock jerking with his pulse, and yes, his toes curling.

"I had no idea!"

No idea? That the anus could grant such pleasure? I shouldn't have been surprised. Poor human males, depriving themselves of such rapture.

His reactions were so erotic I could not help but tongue him for half an hour. I swear he whimpered toward the end, so overcome was he. My tongue began to strain or I would have continued all night.

His muscular ring was sufficiently slackened. I coated him with the lubricant I had near and continued my sensuous massage with my fingers.

"Kali," he said breathless. "That feels amazing."

His cock leaked with dew now. He'd been stiff so long without release I feared he'd get petrified balls. But no, my Richard bore his

pleasure well. He yielded his most reserved place to me in absolute trust.

I pushed my greased index finger easily inside him and his breath caught.

"Is that all right, Richard?"

"It feels fine. I expected it to hurt."

"Could you take a second one?"

"Do whatever you want, Kali."

I swirled my finger inside him, loosening his entrance gently. "What I want is to fuck you."

He grunted and his cock jerked. "If you push for it, I won't resist you. But I'd rather we try that tomorrow."

I got a second finger into him. His stomach muscles tightened, and I heard him groan. I slowly undulated the digits until he relaxed.

"If that's for tomorrow, then what's for tonight?"

"Let me have you."

I smiled. That seemed a prize of equal value, but I wouldn't relinquish his ass just yet. I trained him with the two fingers at length so I'd have an easier time preparing him tomorrow. Somehow I found his sweet spot, and he jolted his body to the side.

"What are you doing! My word!"

That's when I released him. I used the shield of the blanket to lubricate my long-unused bottom and then threw back the sheet so he could see me. Our eyes locked as I straddled him and slowly worked his hard length into me.

"My God, Kali—you're so beautiful."

To stretch myself after so long a break was a nefarious delight. He felt hot inside me. Filling me enough to mash my pulsating place within. I moaned in delirious ecstasy. My nipples hardened.

My cock, which had been erect all through his tonguing, pointed straight to the ceiling.

"You feel so good, Richard."

"Stop it you wicked beast. I'm about to burst!"

I ran my hands over his bare chest while enjoying his girth inside me. Then I inched up, moving his shaft from deep inside, and his face contorted.

"No good, no good, I can't hold back!"

His torso clenched, and he banged his pelvis upwards. Hot seed gushed into me. I closed my eyes, quivering as I received it. His moans were like snarls now. He uttered them through bared teeth while jolting up his hips. Damn, he became pure eroticism when he came.

Richard finished and gasped at me. "That's not how I am usually. It was your tongue. You brought me to the edge. I couldn't help myself."

I dismounted him, freeing his softening cock and a dribble of white issuance. "It's okay, Richard."

"No it isn't." He rolled on top of me and snatched me by my hips. "Get over here."

Without any pause he took my cock in his mouth. I yelped both with shock and searing excitement.

"Oh, Richard!"

He sucked me with the same vigor I'd shown him the night before. Oh, that slippery tongue, teasing the slit at the head of my cock and making me twinge with ecstasy. I wriggled my legs and let out choked moans which just spurred him onward. When I could hold back no longer, I tugged his hair. Richard released me from his mouth with a final suck that made my organ pop

free. Then two pumps of his fist finished me in an embarrassing fit of movement. His mouth, the fact that he did that, it was so erotic I lost all reason.

40 Even More Love

The next night I made love to my sweet Richard for the first time. He rested on his stomach and let me mount him. After an hour of tender preparation, licking, fingering, and coating him thoroughly with lubricant, I slowly pressed inside him.

I can't describe in words how meaningful it was for Richard to give himself to me. He is the one true love of my life. He loved me enough in return that he let me inside him, something most human men will claim is fiendish.

Richard braced his body for me, received my organ, and gave me cues with his staggered breaths for when I could proceed. He was quaking beneath me, his eyes closed, his entire being transfixed by what was happening to him.

When it felt good he twitched and said my name, reaching back to take my hand.

"Don't let me hurt you, Richard."

"It only hurts a little. It…it's beautiful in a way. I feel such warmth in my middle. Like joy that's going to make me cry. I love you so dearly."

His tears didn't come, but mine did. I closed over his body, kissing his neck and connecting to him flesh to flesh. Richard was a more mystical creature than any faun. He was a human man that let himself be loved by another.

When I was finished, spent but still overcome with blissful emotion, he asked if he could make love to me in return. I kissed him and gave my body as easily as I had before. I adored how Richard fucked me, so virile and passionate.

Our rented room turned into our sanctuary of love. We were both eager to join our bodies. Richard became able to endure my member without any pain. He admitted he loved it. How many nights did he growl for me to thrust harder into him? How many times did he buck against my cock, desperate to feel me deeper? Too many to count.

He made love to me with equal passion that it was always sublime. I let my quavering breath be heard, my soft moans to be choked in my throat. His every caress made me flush with orgasmic tingles.

We honeymooned in absolute bliss, hypnotized by our love. I swear it poured from our very skin, igniting the air in our small room. To be with him was to feel rapture. Not just when we made love, but at all times. When we spoke. When our hands roamed easily over each other. We would feed each other treats we brought home like silly lovesick teenagers.

The only thing that could break us from our haze of ecstasy was the need to start rehearsing for the next play. Richard got systems in place to create better sets, obtain better costumes, and our acting troupe doubled in size. We put up 300 pounds to build the production for there was no doubt we would easily recoup it.

The new play was an extravagant epic, worthy of the stardom we'd built up in our last show. I felt the story was less special than Midwinter Love. The romance was braced on a war story that took up many of the scenes. What would save it for me was the final act, after the characters Richard and I played escaped together, and he pulled off my dress to lie me down and make love to me. This would be the reveal of my legs, and the

climax to a gripping love story. I became excited whenever the time came for us to rehearse that scene.

Two weeks of the show was sold out before our first curtain call. Then we had both full matinees and evening shows. The King's Papers once again gave a glowing review, but with a requisite criticism: 'there was less of Kali on the stage than in the last production, and he's the reason we all go to the shows.'

This time we were booked for a solid season, from September to November. The manager harangued us to put on another show for the spring. We'd learned he didn't get fifty pounds from other shows, but merely five pence a seat, and seats often didn't sell out. We had no plans for our next show, no idea what it would be. Richard told him we'd think about it.

We snuggled together on our bed the night after our last show of The General's Daughter.

"What do you think? Should we put on a show for spring? That gives us most of the winter off."

I pouted. "We don't need the money, and the theater will still be cold."

He smiled at me. "How much money do we have, Kali?"

"More than fifteen thousand pounds."

"My word. That's enough to retire forever."

"Not forever. But let's not put on another show until next summer."

He squeezed me and kissed my forehead. "You wish is my command. This sounds like a good time to write that memoir."

I pursed my lips. "Do you think I should?"

"That ass Colby already told the city your land is more debauched than ours. It certainly didn't hurt ticket sales."

"But if I speak of all the men I've slept with, they'll deduce I'm sleeping with you, as well."

"No, no. I meant to tell you this. Don't write about the homosexuality. Make the men you slept with women. Like that teacher you told me about. Have him be a matron instead of a man."

I groaned. "I'd rather not write it at all if I have to twist things. How would that make sense when I get to the part about the brothel? Women don't hire prostitutes."

He wet his lips. "Yes, about that part, I'd have you say you worked in the mines instead. I don't want our fans looking at you through a warped lens. They don't know you as I do."

"I'm not writing it, Richard. What you suggest is stupid. If I change things that much I may as well write fiction, and I have no desire to do that. The memoir would have kept my interest because it was a true record of my life, particularly my time with you. If I have to make up half the story I don't want to write it at all."

Richard thought it over with a deep breath. "I'd actually like to read your true history. You've told me a great deal, but I want to know more." He patted my shoulder while staring at the ceiling. "How about this? You write the real story. Hold nothing back. Don't censor yourself. Think of it as being just for me. We'll keep that copy private. I'll take it and rewrite all the parts I think we need to. That's what will give to the publisher."

I grumbled. "I wish there was some way my real story could be published."

"Kali, you know that would—"

"I know, Richard. I'll do what you say. I just don't like the thought of putting out a deceitful memoir."

I set up the desk the next day with all the necessities for my burgeoning writing career: pen and paper, coffee, salty crackers from my favorite bakery, and menth which was a stimulant people here insufflated that I occasionally used to maintain my energy while part of a show.

I began to write my story, but it went slow, so very slow. A month passed with only one chapter to show for it. I wrote the true story as Richard had advised me, but with every sentence I wondered what my words would be transformed into. What would make it to the final publication? Knowing my words would not remain true both frustrated and inhibited me. More than once I thought of giving up.

Richard reading my work encouraged me. He absorbed every word like succor, riveted by my story. With him as my patron I was able to manage three chapters before spring.

In spring my writing went on hiatus because Richard couldn't resist returning to the stage after winter. His restlessness and the financial needs of some of our actors got us to start Temperance a season earlier than I'd wanted. I acquiesced to this development because I'd gotten a bit restless too and wanted a break from struggling to write.

Temperance was our third production and by now you'd think we'd begin to flag. Not at all. I was the in the titular role to the delight of the King's Paper reviewer and mesmerized the audience in almost every scene. We always sold out both the matinees and evening shows. The manager wanted for us to do two seasons of this

same show. Richard, with his savvy instincts, refused to go even one month over the current season. He had estimated the maximum crowds and felt we'd have empty seats if we persisted.

We planned and projected so smugly as if everything were going to be wonderful forever. In truth we didn't even make it through the full production of Temperance.

41 Running

While still in the midst of Temperance we made an absolutely abhorrent mistake, and I was all to blame. I still have trouble forgiving myself.

I had a favorite bakery that would release a new kind of treat each month. On the first day the treat would always be sold out, which was normally fine because I didn't care for sweets. A few times however, they produced the most delicious savory vegetable pies. I saw the poster for the upcoming treat on my Tuesday off and nearly swooned. They were coming out with a spinach pie with the kind of papery crust I adored. I demanded we run off before the show and purchase a slice on the day of its release. Alas, it was sold out by the time we came to the head of the line.

The baker heard that we'd come looking for his treat and had tickets for our show that night. He brought half a pie and when Richard presented me a slice back stage, I couldn't resist kissing him passionately in jubilation.

We were seen by a woman brought into the production to play a maid with only two lines. Neither Richard nor I thought anything of it. We were her employers, and perhaps she didn't see what she thought she saw. At any rate, Richard and I kissed on the stage frequently with no consequences. We presumed the same could be said back stage.

That next afternoon, however, on our day off, Colby was once again camped before our door. I thought the reporter was there to badger me about the memoir once more. His dour face said otherwise.

"Please, I must talk to you, and we haven't a moment to lose."

We let the panicked man in, but he never took a seat. He handed Richard a page from the King's Papers. I leaned over his shoulder to read.

Kali the Faun and Lead Actor Richard Homosexual Lovers

Oh, how my heart sank.

The rest of the article was no better than this horrifying title. Our passionate kiss had exposed us and was bolstered by the previous revelation of how sexual my home land was.

Richard's face went red. "Did this go out today?" The question came as a furious shout.

"No. This is tomorrow's front page. It's in the printer now. I just couldn't...I mean...if I saw the two of you brought to the executioner, I just couldn't live with myself. This is all the head start I can give you. The magistrate's don't know. Get out of the city tonight. It's your only chance."

"Oh dear God. Kali! Get the money together!"

I ran to my first stash to obey.

Richard put his hand on Colby's shoulder and raced him out the door. "Thank you. You've saved our lives and we won't forget it. We'll send you that memoir through a private courier."

"You will?"

"Yes. Now get out!"

He thrust the man out and began frantically emptying drawers on our mattress. He dumped out my jewelry chest next. The he froze and put a hand to his forehead.

"Stop. Stop, Kali."

I halted with my arms full of bundled paper pound notes.

"We can't lose our minds now. We have all night to get away. Let's think. What are we doing?"

"Taking the wagon out of here."

"We can't take the wagon. It will be too slow! We need to get the horses. Where are the horses?"

"In the rented stable across town."

"Then we need to hire a carriage."

I dropped the pile of money on the bed. "This is all of it. I'm going to the street to beckon a carriage before it gets dark."

"Right. Go." He pulled a satchel out from under the bed and stuffed it with jewels and money.

Once I had a carriage rented, I was able to return to help him while the driver waited.

"Two bags. That's all we can take. What can you not bear to leave behind, Kali?"

"Just you. I don't care about anything else."

"Then we'll just take your jewels and the money." As he said this, he threw me my cloak and put on his long waist coat. "And the memoir." He snatched my pages from my desk. We each pulled a heavy bulging satchel over our shoulder and ran to the carriage.

Richard stopped halfway down the walk. I paused to look back at him.

"We need the canvas from the wagon. It might be our only shelter. And blankets—we need to plan for the cold nights. Damn it, we don't have the saddles and bridles for the horses!"

I went back to him and placed my hands on his chest to calm him. "We'll buy the gear at the stable, then we'll ride to the next town and get whatever else we need there."

"Right." He ran a hand through the hair at my temple. "We'll be okay, Kali."

I managed a smile for him. "I know, Richard."

Oh, how we ran those horses ragged. It was dawn when we reached Applewaithe and we paid extra for two stable bays at the inn for them to get double food and water. We cloistered ourselves in our own room and tried to sleep.

Two hours later, when I was just beginning to slumber, someone knocked at the door. Richard bolted up so furious I thought the bed frame would collapse.

"Who is it? What do you want?"

"Oh…er, sorry m'lord. I just came to see if you'd be ordering breakfast."

"We don't want anything! Go away!"

"Richard."

My manic lover turned to me.

"We have to keep up our strength."

He sighed and rubbed his hand over his face. "Okay, I'm sorry. Bring up two breakfasts for us."

"What will you be having m'lord."

"Everything. Just bring up a feast."

"Oh! Yes, m'lord. Right away."

He returned to the rickety bed and slumped down. I crawled near to rub his shoulders. His tendons were hard as steel.

"I'm so sorry for this, my love."

He put his hand on mine. "It's all right Kali."

I fought back tears.

Richard glanced back at me. "We're rich. That's the best way to be on the run."

I nodded with pursed lips. A tear broke free on my cheek.

Richard pulled me into his arms. "No, no, no, my love. Everything's going to be fine. We'll take new names and start a new life for ourselves."

"We can't."

"Of course we can."

I pulled free from him. "We can't. A new name won't get rid of my horns, legs, and tail."

His lower lip quivered. He turned away from me. "Then…then we'll leave the country. We'll get on a ship. Sail to Morretta."

"Isn't that where the cannibals are from?"

"Somewhere else then."

We both became silent. Minutes later the steward returned with a rolling tray holding our feast. Richard gave him one of our paper pounds and refused to get change.

"Thank you, m'lord! Is there anything else I can get you?"

"Yes. A copy of the King's Papers."

"Oh, that? Yes, sir. Right away."

The boy ran off. Richard waited for him in front of the door. He exchanged a look with me, straining to form a smile.

The steward returned and gave him the paper.

"Is this the most recent copy you have?"

"Yes, m'lord. That's the latest we have. We'll get a newer copy this evening, but it takes a good four days for the latest paper to come in from the courier service."

"Ah. I see. Well, thank you."

"It's two pence for the paper, m'lord, but I'll just have it out of the change for your breakfast. You know breakfast was only a quarter, even a feast like that. You sure you don't want any change back?"

"No. Just bring me the new paper when it arrives."

"Yes, m'lord! I'll come up as soon as it gets in."

Richard closed him out and returned to the bed. He handed me the five day old paper.

"We're safe, Kali."

I wanted to mention a traveler from the capital might bring the newest paper with him, but the inn was nearly vacant. It didn't seem likely.

Richard brought the tray over. It had a full loaf of brown bread, cold roasted partridge, peeled hard boiled eggs, boiled cabbage, roasted potatoes, a pitcher of ale and a pitcher of water. The drinks were cold from basement storage.

I took a few bites of bread and soon found my appetite. Richard tore into the partridge.

"We'll stay today and tonight and leave tomorrow morning. That will get the horses rested, and it's only a half day's ride to Dursby."

"We're going west?"

"We've gone west, yes. The only close town east of the capital was Maisie's home. I'm too well known there. There isn't much to the south of us, and north is the sea. This is the route I know best." He took a deep breath. "We'll need to keep ahead of the paper, which shouldn't be too hard. Eventually there will be wanted posters for us all over the country. Our only real option is Easton. That's a big enough city for us to hide in."

I stared at him. Hiding anywhere with me was impossible, or it meant my living in a closet. Easton couldn't be our only option.

Then I had an epiphany.

"Richard. Let's go to my land."

He blinked at me.

"Let's go all the way back to the death cliffs, find my passage way, and escape to my home."

He felt his chin in consideration, then looked at me. "Our money is worthless there."

"Trade the money for gold. Gold is as valuable there as it is here."

"Is that right?" His tenor had lifted.

"And you would become the attraction in my land. We've never heard of humans. We could start a carnival over there."

His face brightened. "My God."

"And we wouldn't have to love each other in secret. We could be married in Schaletar."

"Kali! That's magnificent!" He hugged me and gave me a kiss. "But can you find that passage again? Can we still get through it?"

"Take me back to where you camped when you first found me and I'll bring you to the passage. It hasn't been that long. I'm sure we can still get through."

"Oh, Kali, yes! Yes!" He hugged me once more. "You've given me my life back!"

"It's only fair," I said, tearful while I clung to him. "I'm the one who ruined it."

"I would go to your land even if we hadn't been ruined. Think of the adventure! And this time you can be my guide. You'll be the carnival master and I'll be the attraction."

I laughed, and this time spilled tears of joy.

He wiped away my tear with his thumb. "I don't care if I lose my whole world. As long as I have you I'll be happy."

"You'll be happy in my home too, Richard. It's just as fine as the human world and twice as free."

"I believe you." He soothed my face. "Oh, Kali, I'm sure of it!"

We ate our feast with joy then. The next few hours were filled with talk of faun carnivals. I told him about our different clowns and the magic acts I'd seen. He got giddy at my descriptions.

We slept part of the day and through the night. Richard got up before it was light and I went with him to retrieve our horses. For now the plan was still to go to Easton because that's where we could buy one ounce gold coins that would be easy to carry into my land. We were still at risk so long as we were in Richard's world. This prevented us from celebrating in full.

I had hope again, however. I knew we had a magnificent life ahead of us.

42 Schaletar

And so, with our satchels now filled with heavy gold coins, two new canteens of water, and after releasing our two horses near a brook, we climbed up the hill to the passage. A tree blocked it with branches that had to be scraped past to get in. Inside I saw the dim light at the other end. Our path to salvation was still clear.

"I can see why no one discovered this on our end. No one has a reason to come out this far unless they're looking for a centerus." Richard stared at the opening on his side before we went further. "Still, I'd like to block it. What if someone comes through looking to hunt us?"

"They'd never find us. We're going to emerge far away from the land of the centeri, then we have to travel a great deal to get back to the land of the fauns. There's hundreds of villages where we could be."

Richard climbed back out. "We'll be famous in your realm soon and easy to hunt. If not that you'll have missionaries coming through thinking to convert you. They're followed by conquerors who consider you subhuman because of your different morals." He found a rock and pulled it behind him back into the crevice. "No, Kali. I think I want our worlds to remain separate."

The rock, which was the size of a baby, hid the passage even more. And tree branches pushed against it making it arduous to remove from the other side. Richard was satisfied, and we proceeded.

The trip back to Calico was an ordeal because we wouldn't abandon our hundred pounds of gold for anything. I also wasn't sure which way

to go. I headed east and prayed the woods would end and a town would appear. We had to sleep outside two nights. Other than weeds we had nothing to eat.

Richard remained upbeat. He said we'd last forever just on water.

The outer limits of Calico finally appeared. We followed a trail to a dirt road and saw people and businesses far ahead of us.

I took off my cloak and gave it to Richard.

"It's your turn to be concealed."

"Really? What will happen if they see me?"

"I was robbed in this town, so you might be kidnapped. At the very least it will be a nuisance. I don't have good memories here. I want to leave as fast as we can."

He donned the cloak but was able to keep the hood down since centeri have no horns. As weary as we were Richard still erupted with joyful laughter at the sight of the horse-men.

"Dear God, look at them all. They were here all this time, barely a hundred miles away from us."

"Centeri are a novelty in my land. They still make good carnival attractions." I grinned at him. "Nothing like a human, though."

The apothecary was where we bought nuts and bread for our first bite of food. We chose this place to break our fast because it had a counter where you could sell gold. I only parted with one of our coins since they were more valuable near my home. An ounce of bullion gave us thirty coin. I walked away from the window to join Richard at a bench he'd dropped himself outside.

"Thirty coin?" he said. "How much can that buy us?"

"A coin is worth a little more than a pound."

His eyes bulged. "We've got over three thousand coins. You're telling me they're worth thirty pounds each?"

"No. They're worth more than that, because gold in Schaletar is much rarer than Calico. We might get forty coin an ounce there."

Richard grabbed the scruff of my shirt. "Are you telling me we're rich?"

"Rich as a king." I whispered this. "But only if we aren't robbed."

As much as I loathed it, we had to spend a night at the inn where I'd worked. We ate, we rested, and were still devastated from our time in the woods. I only emerged from our room because I wanted to see who was the comfort worker. It was still Gabin, only now he took red cards because Soan had gently initiated him. He looked well, so did Camille and Ethan. I didn't try to find Mrs. Alita since I didn't want to be badgered about coming to work for her again.

The next day we trekked another 20 miles, still not fully recovered from the woods, but propelled onward by my firm desire to get out of Calico. I finally got on the carriage that would take me to Trummel. I'd closed the circle I'd left open two years ago.

Trummel was Richard's first glimpse of faun society and he was elated, but I insisted we continue to Schaletar. That was my home, where I knew the people and places, and where I felt safe. It was agreed we'd head there the next day.

That evening we went to the bank and sold the rest of our gold for close to 73,000 coin. It was too much money to withdraw so Richard and I claimed to be married and opened a joint account. I

requested this account be moved to the bank in Schaletar. We left with only five coin each, plenty of money to sustain us.

We had a grand dinner (the first of which where Richard complained about the lack of meat) then secured a room at Trummel's fine inn for two shillings, which I explained to Richard equaled forty pennies.

In the room I marveled at the figure in our bank book. "The bank gives us interest of 3% a year. That's over two thousand coin. We could live on a fourth of that."

Richard snuggled next to me. "It's nice to come into your world as wealthy people. Isn't that better than how you came into mine?"

I smiled at him. "I would do it all over without a thought. It was worth it to find you."

Richard soothed my hair. His touch still gave me flutters in my core.

"I remember when I first saw you. You were the most beautiful creature I'd ever beheld. Then I cursed the fact that you were male—this even while I had a wife."

"Do you still curse it?"

He kissed me. "No. I wouldn't want you any other way."

I floated on the bliss of his words while staring into his vivid eyes.

"But you aren't seriously thinking of just living on our interest, are you? We have a carnival to build."

I laughed. Of course Richard would not be satisfied with retirement. I intended to lock a hearty sum of our money away from his reach, to be certain we'd never want for anything again.

The next day we were in Schaletar, and I had tears of joy as my old main street came into view. I dropped us off at the square and showed Richard the place where the carnival I'd seen set up years ago.

"Why this is just the same as in my world. We can go back to our old life, Kali!"

I drew a breath through my nostrils. "Was traveling better than putting on shows in the theater?"

He looked around the grassy square. "No. I was happiest in the capital, enjoying all the riches of the city with you on my arm."

"Not on your arm. I couldn't dare hold on to you in public."

He smiled. "I will finally concede your people's values are superior. Not that I've seen much of them yet. If people are fucking in the markets like you say they do, I might think differently."

I took his hand. "Just turn away."

We walked to Schaletar's theater, which was a far smaller affair than the one in the capital. It could seat fifty people and currently had a show of shadow puppets running. Richard found it odd.

"Do you think they'd like Midwinter Love here?"

"It would be spectacular, but you realize you would have to play Jawlee and I would play Morco."

"Ha! So in your land I become the woman."

I curled my arm around him. "Aren't we both versatile?

He reciprocated my embrace. "We are indeed. You made me that way." He took a deep

breath that made his chest rise and fall. "But I think your home town is too small for us, Kali."

I swallowed. "I know. North of Trummel is Dianbys, the capital. I've never been there, but I hear it's gigantic. I'm sure there's a fine theater for us to try out there."

"And cafes and bakeries?"

"Probably."

"Then we'll go there, won't we? Become the toast of a new city?"

My gaze went downward. "Why don't we stay awhile here first? I think I've missed it."

"And we haven't had our season off."

I nodded. "And I'd like to finish writing that memoir. You promised Colby he'd have it."

"I did...but that's before I knew we were leaving the human world."

"Can't we still get it to him? We could hire a courier in Claybridge."

He considered. "If you write it, I'll get it to the publisher. At least now you don't have to censor yourself."

I hugged my body against his side. "Thank you!"

And if all went well, dear reader, you have my book in your hand. I know not how much my publisher will censor it, nor do I know if I've left too many clues for you to find my passage. (You can be certain I changed some details to keep it hidden.)

After Richard gets the manuscript to a courier we shall go to Diansby to revive the life we had in the capital. If we fail, all is well. We have all the money we could need for a dozen life times.

Best of all, however, we have each other.

The End.

43 A Note From King's Paper Publishing House

Thank you for your purchase of *The Decadent Life of a Faun.* This manuscript was delivered to us three years ago, and we presumed we would hold it indefinitely without ever bringing it to publication.

The primary reason for this was the notorious description of the behavior of Earl Chantwell. After his public scandal and subsequent execution we approached our patron, the most reverent King Artimas, and sought permission to proceed with publication.

The king's ministers reviewed this memoir at length and said for us to publish it without censoring the contents.

After reading the most salacious descriptions found herein, this fact may come to you as a great surprise. Our shock came from the fact that the description of the king's after-festival party contained some licentious material that was allowed to go to print.

The king's high ministers said that his majesty holds chaste and formal parties, and those who were described to be copulating with doors open or running about in states of nudity, are not members of his court, but the lower-ranking nobles who are right to be shamed.

As for the other lurid descriptions of sex acts his majesty wished for this to be presented in its purity for the book is the only record, our society has of a faun and faun-kind. To censor this would be a disservice to future explorers who require an accurate record to proceed with.

It was further stated that thought the carnival master Richard could not resist a descent into carnality; he had insight that is worth promoting. We must not judge other species and races using our ethics as a guide, but must rather understand their society and what has caused their values to veer from those we know to be correct.

In the case of the fauns it was the manner of estrus described by the author Kali. Should the clergy ever wish to make missions into the faunland they must have understanding for the reasons behind their deviation of values order to redeem them.

Though a large percentage of this memoir contains salacious content, it can not be denied that the faun Kali presented as a sophisticated and intelligent character who was able to assimilated, albeit briefly, into the city life of Mintbridge. It could be presumed that other fauns would also integrate and continue to present us insight about their society. It is further presumed that the depiction of the faunland was accurate, and that humans might travel there without any greater fear of bodily harm than that which we would find in our own boroughs.

The Decadent Life of a Faun is sold without restriction throughout Mintbridge, Easton, and the greater townships where bookstores are present. If a magistrate discovers this book in your home please refer him to this page. The benefits of sharing this book with the population was deemed to have outweighed the detriments, as deemed by our noble King Artimas.

44 Author Yamila's Note

This is the longest novel I've written and it poured straight from my soul onto the page. I hope this experiment is a success, and that you enjoyed Faunication. I hope you found it even worthy of a 5 star review. All reviews are useful to me, even short 'it was good' reviews help me tremendously. Please take a moment to leave one.

I love to connect with my fans on social media!

My web site: http://yamilaabraham.com
My Tumblr: http://yaoipress.com
My Webcomics: http://yaoimila.com
My FB Page: https://www.facebook.com/Yaoimila/
My FB Group: https://www.facebook.com/groups/1669766673294234/
Yaoi FB Page: https://www.facebook.com/theyaoist/
My Twitter: https://twitter.com/yaoipress
My Pinterest: https://www.pinterest.com/yaoipress/
My Google+: https://plus.google.com/+YaoiPress/
My Email: yaoimila@gmail.com

Dear Friends, *please don't share this ebook online!* Piracy has devastated my ability to make a living in the past. *I beg you* to please not post this or any of my works online. Thanks so much to

everyone who has supported me with a legal purchase!

Newsletter Subscription

FREE EBOOK!

Click Here to Subscribe to
Yamila Abraham's Newsletter
and get a Complete Stand-Alone
Male/Male Romance Novel
Free!

You'll Get Free Release Notifications, Special
Offers, Discounts, and More!
To sign up follow this link:
http://eepurl.com/bgZgVv

45 Other Works

Sensitive: Yaoi Hentai Gay Erotic Fantasy

Sen has no memory of the castle he's in or the princess he's about to marry. Things grow even more confusing when the handsome demon god Lilivite shows up to kidnap his bride. He claims Sen was his lover, and if he wants to leave him for this woman he'll have to go to his dark realm and rescue her.

Somehow, Sen knows it's the truth. Nothing makes sense except what he felt when he saw the demon Lilivite. He'll go to the dark realm, rumored to have energies so perverse men die of exhaustion when they dare enter, and find his answers from the demon who so compels him.

Loaded with yaoi hentai scenes, male/male loving, touching romance, and a mystery to be unraveled. A full novel in one installment with a guaranteed HEA!

FREE on Kindle Unlimited!

Click your country to grab it now!

Kindle USA, Kindle UK, Kindle Germany, Kindle Australia, Kindle Canada, Kindle France, Kindle Italy, Kindle Spain, Kindle Brazil, Kindle Mexico, Kindle Netherlands, Kindle Japan, or Kindle India!

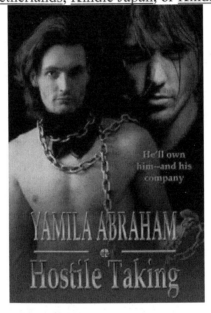

Hostile Taking

Traumatized father Merrick has a business that's about to fail. That means both _him_ and his company will be claimed by a 'Mentor.' This riveting and spicy sci-fi romance has a guaranteed HEA and is presented in its entirety in a single installment. _This is not a series._ By the author of The Eidolon's Conquest!

Free on Kindle Unlimited!

Click your country to grab it now! Kindle USA, Kindle UK, Kindle Germany, Kindle Canada, Kindle Australia, Kindle France, Kindle Italy, Kindle Spain, Kindle Mexico, Kindle Japan, Kindle India, Kindle Netherlands, or Kindle Brazil!

46 Glossary

Fauns: In this story fauns are half human and half sheep. Go Back

Satyr: In this story satyrs are half human and half goat. Go Back